Disclaimer

This is a work of historical fiction. Names, characters, organisations, places, events, locales, and incidents are either the products of the author's imagination or used in a fictitious manner. Any resemblance to actual persons, living or dead, or actual events is purely coincidental.

info@thelostgraillegends.co.uk
www.thelostgraillegends.co.uk

Original artwork by Morgan Guige
Map designs by Vadim Ever
Edited by Melanie Scott

Dedication

This book is dedicated to my mother, Rosamond Anne Jones, who first introduced me to the legend of the Grail Quest.

'Mum, on our trips to Renne le Chateaux and Jerusalem when I was just a small boy, you sparked an interest in me that never died. Your life was a clear demonstration of what it is to live in grace, and through terrible misfortune, you also showed me how to die bravely, steadfast in courage. I love you, I miss you, and I hope I will see you again one day. I never knew how special you were until you were gone.'

Table of Contents

Matthew 7:7
Ask, and it will be given to you;
seek, and you shall find;
knock, and it will be opened to you.

Foreword

The following novel represents a lifetime of personal interest, culminating in three years of perplexing work as I attempted to assemble this fascinating puzzle together. Inside this book, you will find a series of twenty short stories that will take you on a time-travelling journey of discovery, through myth, legend, and history. We will now discover a series of forgotten events that are set in, on and around Hamsey, an ancient piece of unassuming land in the heart of the Sussex Downlands. This is an astonishing place, with an astonishing story to tell. I present to you, The Lost Grail Legends of Lewes and Hamsey...

Joseph and Jeshua
Year 07

Chapter - 1

Joseph and Jeshua
Year 07

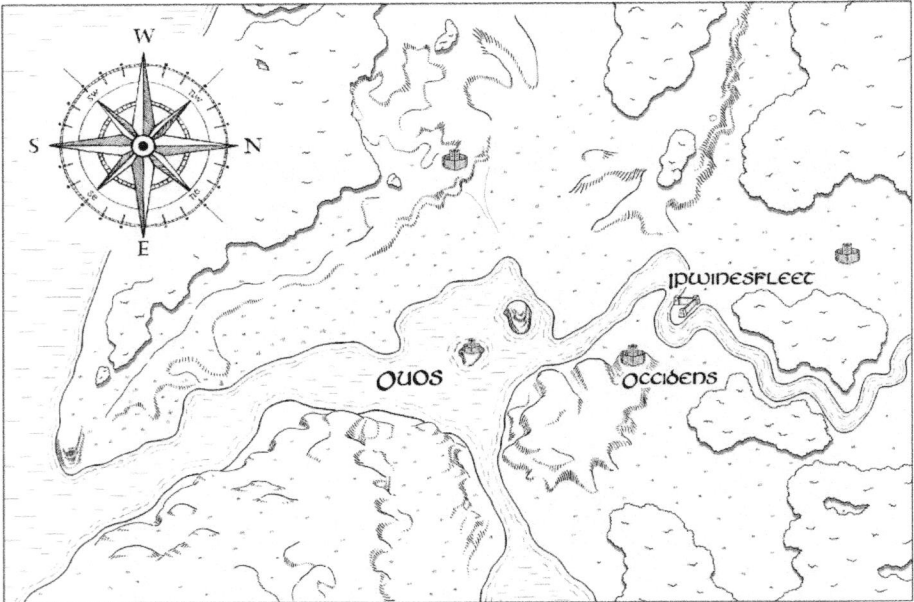

'Come here to me, child, and hold fast to the rigging!'

The ship's timbers groaned as the small sailing vessel climbed another steep wave. The storm had come upon them suddenly, the sky blackening from the east, swiftly followed by high winds and a deep swell in the ocean; but Joseph was an experienced sailor. He had travelled far and wide in his young life, establishing himself as a wealthy man by taking risks that others would not; journeying to far-off lands and trading in refined metals. He had quickly learned the difference in value an ingot could accrue by simply moving it from one location to another, and Joseph had been born with a natural affinity for numbers. The challenge was often in surviving the journey, and this crossing from Gaul to the land known as Albion was proving to be no exception. Joseph looked down at his young son, who clung to a thick rope fixed to the foot of the mast. He was surprised to see that Jeshua appeared to be enjoying the dangerous seas; he was also glad that he was showing no sign of the dreaded seasickness that so commonly assailed even experienced men on rough waters.

'Do you fare well, Jeshua?' Joseph inquired of him, shouting above the wild wind and the lashing rain.

Jeshua looked up at him calmly and smiled, nodding his head in affirmation, then turned his attention back to the clouds ahead of them.

'I think it will pass quickly, Father,' he shouted back, pointing to the far distance.

The storm had come upon them with little warning; there had been no sign of danger in the skies when they had departed the Gaulish coast. The seas had been calm, and the winds were in their favour as they had set sail. Joseph turned his gaze to where Jeshua was pointing and thought perhaps he could see a flicker of bright blue on the distant skyline. He could not be sure, but the boy had an uncanny ability to see far further than Joseph was able to, and he had quickly learned to trust his son's sight and instincts; they had aided him greatly over the last two years.

Although this was proving to be a perilous journey, Joseph had decided to bring Jeshua on this trading mission to a place he had never ventured to before, the mysterious island known as Albion. He had been left little choice in the matter, for no living family members were able to care for his son in Nazareth now. Even at his young age, though, Jeshua was an able seaman and, despite his small stature, he proved to be a great aid as they sailed. Joseph was truly glad they were together.

At the Gaulish coast, he had seen the fine quality of the metal that had come from the land across the sea. He had known then that Albion would be his next destination. Joseph sought to purchase high-quality iron ingots from the Roman bloomeries there, and then, if fate was kind, sell them on back in Israel, hopefully for a significant profit. He had already travelled to many lands following the well-established and moderately safe routes the Romans had been creating over the last two centuries, yet this land was on the outer limits of Roman-held territories. Joseph had never ventured so far from home; but if the trip was a success, it would make him an incredibly wealthy man.

He could see it now, he was certain; the blue sky on the horizon. The swell in the waves also seemed to be beginning to drop. Joseph let out a sigh of relief as he became aware of the tightness he had been holding, now easing in his tired limbs. He had to admit that sailing the open ocean was never easy, but despite this, he had always enjoyed the unpredictable adventure. Whilst other folk seemed content to live and die in the repetitive doldrums of home, he had found himself to be happiest living as a nomad. For Joseph, the world seemed so full of diversity and intrigue that to see as much as he could before he died was what he truly lived for. The earth and the seas were alive with magic. He strived to see it all.

The ship sailed on, tacking left and right to counter the driving winds, and while Jeshua manned the tiller, Joseph skilfully worked the sail and the rigging. It was not long before they saw it; a flicker of bright white on the distant horizon. They had been told to look out for this feature, and were informed that if they held a steady course in that direction, they would reach the land known as Albion and the trading port of Ipwinesfleet that the Romans had constructed there in the very recent past. Their only other instruction was to sail left of the white cliffs, past the entrance to the first estuary at their foot. The tidal inlet to the hilltop encampment known as Occidens and the impressive Roman villa of Mutuantonis should be easily located a short distance along the coast from here. The sea had cut an enormous channel inland that the Romans had named the Ouos, and by all accounts, it could not be missed.

The Romans had not been there for long, driven back at first by the fierce and wild Regnii warriors, but the legions were now establishing a strong presence in the land and Joseph had been assured that a safe harbour would await him if he succeeded in his sea crossing. He had heard fanciful tales of druids, sorcery, mists and monsters on his journey around the Gaulish coastline, and it seemed that many of those fanciful tales' origins could be found in this mysterious land he was now fast approaching. He was nervous, but excited to finally see it.

In a short time, he began to pick out more detail, and noticed that the white on the horizon was becoming an enormous cliff of chalk, rising high out of the ocean; a wall of white with seven distinct hills along its top. He was now certain that this was the place he had been looking for and he breathed another great sigh of relief to discover that the storm had not blown them far off course. Once again, luck seemed to be on his side.

They continued along the coastline as instructed until they saw, at last, the vast tidal estuary of the Ouos. It seemed a wondrous, untamed place. There were countless yew, oak and ash trees rising high on the steep hills of the valley cut by the ocean, and on the hill peaks, the Romans had begun constructing gigantic wooden hill forts as they sought to gain a strong foothold in these new lands. Joseph and Jeshua heard the distinct ringing of hammers echoing gently in the distance as the Roman smiths worked the locally smelted iron into the nails they would need to construct those mighty fortresses. It was good to hear the presence of people once again.

Sailing on, they noticed a tiny island rising out of the centre of the sea channel. It seemed to barely surface above the water, but Joseph knew that the tide was high at that time. Roman warships surrounded the small landmass and construction of another wooden fortress was underway there. There seemed little doubt that this would be used to protect the Ouos from the sea, though attack from this front seemed unlikely; the Romans were focusing most of their attention inland, with one of the mightiest armies the world had ever seen at their back.

A watchman shouted a greeting to them. They clearly posed no threat, so no alarm was raised, and he simply waved them past emphatically from the small wooden lookout tower on the island.

They sailed on, and as they began to pass the fort they noticed another, slightly larger island coming into view which had been hidden from their sight until now. It seemed construction of a small wharf was underway there too, but little other activity was taking place, so they turned their attention to the way ahead and carried on up the estuary.

Ipwinesfleet was only a short distance further on. It was located beyond a sharp bend in the channel, on a small jutting promontory of the mainland; a gentle slope on its south side and a steep port wall to the north, constructed with the masterful stonework the Romans had become so famous for. Beyond this, the Ouos curved beautifully around the promontory in another horseshoe bend, then continued on further upstream towards countless freshwater tributaries and the central lands of Albion. Boats of every description filled the harbour, and the grounds surrounding it were a hive of activity.

Joseph looked up. One of the most impressive forts he had ever seen was being constructed on the enormous escarpment to the east of the port. Its gigantic, chalk-faced cliffs were surrounded by the sea here, and must have provided one of the most secure and magnificent sites on the southern shores. There also appeared to be large burial mounds on the summit of the hill and all along its northern slopes. He had seen many similar mounds in other countries on his travels, but these were enormous. Perhaps they housed the remains of the giant men that once roamed this earth, he thought, then quickly turned his attention back to the job at hand; it was time to make their landing.

After a short search, they found a space to dock their vessel amongst the few crowded jetties that were available to them. With nimble feet, Jeshua hopped onto the boardwalk, a sturdy tether in hand, and secured the boat to a robust wooden upright. Joseph dropped the sail and, with great relief, he climbed from the boat to join Jeshua back on solid ground. They smiled fondly at each other as they took in their new surroundings. They had arrived in Albion.

The harbourmaster strode down to meet them and they waved politely at him as he neared.

'Where do you hail from?' he enquired.

Joseph smiled warmly in greeting. 'We have come from Israel by order of the Emperor to procure metals for the army,' he replied. 'He has tasked all traders to undertake this mission and is willing to pay well for metal ingots of high quality. I travelled to the coast of Gaul many years ago and heard tell of this land and the iron available for purchase here.'

The harbourmaster stroked his white beard and nodded his head. 'You've come to the right place, to be certain. The legions have opened many an iron-smelting bloomery in these parts. Most of it ends up here, for sale or for use by the army. The trading post, and the main settlement of Occidens, are atop the hill on the other shore, but I expect you need some rest before you go about your business, do you not, merchant?'

Joseph nodded his head in agreement. 'Indeed, kind sir, it would be good to gain our land legs once again. Our crossing from Gaul was hazardous. A violent storm hit us out at sea.'

The harbourmaster squinted his eyes as he looked out to the horizon. 'Aye, I saw the weather front come in from here. 'Tis often the way on this stretch of ocean. Many a ship's been taken by the weather in these parts. Heavy mists sink in to the sea valley from hot springs located across these hills; they then work their way out to sea. It has doomed many a vessel here in years past. I had never seen the like until I reached these shores. 'Tis a strange land this Albion, to be sure.' He raised his head, and his narrowed eyes scoured the countryside once again, seeking a mystery he could sense in his bones was out there, but that he could not quite fathom.

'Are there any lodgings nearby?' Joseph asked.

The harbourmaster snapped his attention back to Joseph. 'A little further into the valley, and towards that peak over yonder, you'll find a road that leads north. That'll take you straight to a safe Roman outpost; they should have room for you there. Most of the troops are moving on to fight the Welsh. Ferocious bunch they are, but nought have withstood the legions in my lifetime, and I don't right fancy them wild men's chances.' He shook his head slowly and stroked his beard again. 'Your name before you depart, sir?'

'I am Joseph of Arimathea, and this is my son Jeshua.' Joseph gestured proudly to the boy.

The harbourmaster smiled warmly at them. 'Nice to meet you both. You go on now, and I'll take good care of your vessel. She'll be safe here.'

'Your mooring fee?' Joseph enquired.

'Don't you go worrying 'bout no mooring fees, Mr Joseph. No fees for men on the Emperor's business!'

'Thank you, sir.' Joseph was gladdened by their warm reception. 'You have been most kind. We will see you on the morrow.'

'Name's Eligius. You'll find me somewhere on the promontory most of the day if you need assistance.' He tipped his hat, and sauntered off down the wharf to welcome another boat making port.

Joseph tapped Jeshua on his shoulder, pointed up the slope to the path ahead, and raised an inquisitive eyebrow. 'Let's go and see what this land has to offer us, shall we?'

They smiled at one another, then started their journey up the hill to the small track leading through the green woodland beyond.

As they walked on, the sun broke its way through the shifting clouds and dappled light flowed in through the canopy of trees on either side of the road. Birdsong pierced the silence, rising sharply in appreciation of this sudden change in the weather. The air was fresh and clean. Joseph was becoming enthralled by this peaceful and wondrous place, but he was also aware that this land was, for the most part, safe for him and his son now. He wondered if he would have felt the same had he received his welcome from the Regnii people who had occupied this place before the Romans had conquered it. He would never know now, he pondered sadly.

They walked on as the sun continued to rise in the east, passing only one lone man with a pony and cart, who had been transporting provisions to the fortified outpost. He assured them that the settlement was only a little further, and added that he was heading to the port to replenish supplies for the soldiers stationed there. He seemed eager to talk, and promised he would seek them out on his return to the fort.

The day was becoming warm as they approached the deep ditch surrounding the wooden palisade and came at last to the gates of the outpost. A watchman in one of the towers set along the fortifications called down to them.

'State your purpose!'

Joseph waved his papers up to the guard. 'Emperor's business. We are metal traders from across the ocean and are seeking lodgings for the night. The harbourmaster, Eligius, pointed us this way.'

The guard nodded down below him, and the gate-men removed the enormous wooden locking bar and bid them enter. The guards checked their papers and, seeing all was in order, directed them to a simple structure by the western wall. It had two bunks inside the room, with moderately clean blankets for each. Joseph and Jeshua were very grateful for a chance to rest for a short time while they adapted to their new surroundings. They laid down their tired bodies, well relieved to find safe refuge in this mysterious new land.

Joseph awoke slowly from a pleasant dream and saw that the sun was still fairly high, but had begun to dip slowly away to the west. He could hear a muted conversation in the distance and, above that, the rustling of leaves as a gentle warm breeze flowed across the woodland from the south. He rose from his bed and looked out of the window to the courtyard beyond. The buildings inside the fortification were simple wooden structures, but the Romans had not been here for long. He assumed that they were slow to construct permanent buildings until they were confident the land was safe and entirely under their control. It appeared to Joseph that the occupants of this fort had seen recent warfare, judging by the number of grave-sites they had seen grouped outside the walls. It also looked like sections of the walls had been charred by fire in the recent past; the familiar smell of burnt wood caught his nostrils on occasion. He went to Jeshua's side and gently rocked him back to wakefulness. The boy opened his eyes slowly and began to search out his unfamiliar surroundings. He quickly remembered where he was, smiled, stretched, then let out a mighty yawn.

Jeshua was an unusual boy, thought Joseph once again, though he could not deny he was certainly glad of it. Jeshua never complained, and spoke very little. He did not ask endless questions as did so many other children Joseph had encountered. He always seemed to be content, and had not cried once in the last few years. Joseph often recalled that he had not really cried much even as a baby. Jeshua cheerfully observed, and listened intently. He was also very considered before he spoke; but his true gift, it seemed, was simply his very being. Joseph had quickly noticed how people changed when they were in Jeshua's presence. His lightness of character seemed to spread into his surroundings wherever he went. People became happier and calmer whenever they were around him, no matter what mood Jeshua found them in. Thankfully, no one but Joseph had noticed that the boy caused this odd phenomenon, but he doubted now that anyone ever would. He had quickly realized that, despite his worry, people were easily distracted and mostly paid attention to themselves; they were totally unaware of the subtler influences affecting them in life.

Jeshua rose from his bed and joined Joseph to stand in the dappled light pouring in through the window. It was a beautiful day. Autumn was in the air, and nature was readying itself for the long exhale of winter. Birds sang and the trees swayed gently in the breeze coming in from the south. It was so full of life, this land of Albion; rich and green, with woodland stretching as far as the eye could see. There were mighty oaks, ash, yew, birch, hazel, willow and poplar trees, along with many more species Joseph had never seen before. It seemed a heavenly paradise when compared with the scorching heat and sands of home. That place had its own magic, it was true, but this land was so verdant; even the hills seemed full of life here.

They tidied their beds, gathered their belongings, put on their sandals and stepped out into the warmth of the day. Three beautiful red-breasted birds flew from the roof as the door closed; they did not know their name. Jeshua smiled at the little creatures as the two travellers made their way over to a well located in the centre of the encampment. They drew a bucket up from the depths, had a drink, washed their faces and filled their skins. The water was cold, clean and good. They were now ready to see what the rest of the day would bring them.

The trader they had met on the way in had now reappeared from his trip to the port and was waving excitedly as he made his way over to them. He seemed a friendly, hard-working fellow. Joseph smiled at him warmly as he neared.

'How fares you, Joseph?' asked the trader, remembering his name from their first encounter.

'We are well, thank you, tradesman. Please forgive me, but I did not ask your name?'

'My name is Mathias,' the merchant replied. 'Beautiful day, is it not? I wonder if you would care to join me for luncheon, sirs? I have bread, fish, cold meats and some apples I would share in exchange for news of the outside world, if you would be willing?'

'That would be most gracious of you,' Joseph agreed happily.

'Come then, join me.' The trader waved them over to his cart, and they saw that, set behind it, there was a small lodging in the corner of the fortification. It had a low table, a single sleeping area and some simple furnishings. Mathias went inside and returned with a large rug, which he laid out for them to sit on. Next, he brought out the little table and some small cushions, and began to lay out the lunch he had promised, along with a large clay jug, which he filled with water from the well. It was all very fresh, the meat was well cooked, and they thanked him profusely for his generosity as they sat together and ate with their hands.

They were both very grateful for that meal. Neither Joseph nor Jeshua had eaten properly in many days, and surviving on dry oats and water was never a particularly enjoyable way to live. Hunger is certainly the greatest teacher for gratitude, mused Joseph, as he savoured the crisp apple he was finishing his meal with. Sadly, they did not grow well in Israel, so apples were not commonly found there. Joseph, however, had been lucky enough to taste many varieties on his travels, but this golden apple was one the sweetest he had ever tasted.

As best as he could, Joseph informed Mathias of the goings-on in the world that he had witnessed on his travels to Albion, and Mathias marvelled at Joseph's descriptions of the mighty buildings the Romans had been constructing. The road network was also growing fast, he informed him, and the Empire was flourishing. Joseph then explained his purpose for being in Albion. Mathias gave him directions to the trading post on the other side of the estuary, instructing him to talk with a man called Flavius there, as he was certain that he would have access to the finest quality iron ingots from the surrounding mines. He offered to accompany them back to the wharf the next morning, and Joseph happily agreed. Together, they cleaned up the remains of their luncheon and then talked late into the evening.

The next morning, Eligius, the harbourmaster, welcomed them back warmly as they arrived once more at the port of Ipwinesfleet. Seagulls were swooping in toward a small boat unloading its catch of fish by the wharf, and the fisherman's son was cheerfully chasing them off with a broom while the fish were sorted and set out for sale. It was obviously a daily battle, and the child had learned to turn it into a game. They watched the scene for a short while, much amused by the boy's enthusiasm.

Eligius informed them that Joseph's boat was safe and that there was little to report. They thanked him and Mathias for their kindness, and Joseph insisted on giving them both some silver coins for their assistance; promising he would seek them on his return if he ever made it back to these shores. They generously refused his money. Joseph and Jeshua embraced them with good cheer, feeling that it was the beginning of a long friendship, then boarded their vessel to cross to the other shore. It was a very short distance; the tide was high and so Joseph fixed on the oars, then rowed the small sailing boat across the channel, slowly, but with little effort.

Joseph and Jeshua arrived on the far shore and secured their boat once again. With much enthusiasm, they began their journey along the path that skirted the foot of the enormous steep-sided hill to their left. The sea estuary was to their right and, rising up from the far shore, they glimpsed the small Roman encampments across the channel, slowly spreading inland as the land surveyors laid out the new borders for the town of Mutuantonis. At the bottom of a moderate slope, and right next to the shores of the estuary, they turned left and entered an impressive valley at the foot of the hill. They continued along a narrow trail here until they came to a Y-shaped junction intersecting another incredibly steep rise in its centre, and they looked up to the summit. A mighty bird was flying high above them, soaring in the warm air rising up through the valley. Its screeching call echoed out to them as they forged ahead.

They were both out of breath as they made their way up the left-hand trail to the hilltop, but once they had reached the summit, they turned and saw that the view before them was absolutely stunning. This was an Eden unlike any they had seen before, and the hilltop appeared to be a natural fortification unlike any other in the land. Wherever the sea met this remarkable landmass, it was steep-sided, and virtually impossible to climb.

It seemed that the only visible way up to the summit from the sea was the valley entrance they had just ascended. This made the fort and small town forming along the western ridge one of the most defensible spots on the southern coast. It had likely cost many Roman lives to take that land, but Joseph had seen first-hand what the Roman army was capable of, and he was little surprised that they had eventually won the hilltop from the Regnii people. The green and heavily wooded land upon the rise was vast, and Mathias had informed them that another mighty fort was being constructed atop an even higher peak on its far side, to protect from land invasion from the east.

They followed the ridge back along the valley to the left, quickly locating the trading post within the partially constructed fort walls. They asked for Flavius, as Mathias had instructed, and were informed that he was not there presently, but that he should be returning at any moment, so they sat outside the gates and waited for him, taking in the extraordinary view for a while.

Before long, a golden-haired, well-built man with a noble yet friendly bearing approached them from the woodland trail. Joseph was sure that this was the man he sought, and got up to intercept him.

'Might you be Flavius?' Joseph enquired.

'I am,' the man replied suspiciously, halting mid-stride. 'And who might you be, sir?'

'My name is Joseph. We met a man named Mathias on the far shore who directed us over to you. I am a merchant from the land of Israel. I seek to purchase iron ingots here. The Emperor is offering fair prices for metals of good quality and I heard tell that you might be the man to speak to?'

Flavius relaxed and smiled. 'Ah, Mathias, eh? He's a good man, to be certain, and he has indeed pointed you to the right place. Some very poor quality metals come in from many of the mines in the area, but some are pure and well-refined, and these are the only ingots I will purchase. I will show you some examples, should you wish?'

They shook hands and Flavius ushered them back through the wooden gates. Once inside the fortification, he entered the trading post and, moments later, returned with some iron ingots, and some samples of what looked like another metal in his free hand.

'Here you are,' said Flavius, as he passed Joseph the samples of iron for him to inspect.

Joseph was impressed with the quality. It seemed the smelting process for these ingots had achieved a fairly clean result, with few visible impurities.

'I thought you might like to have a look at this as well,' Flavius offered. He passed Joseph the other ingots he was holding. 'Tin, from the mines in Cornwallium. There are incredibly rich veins of it to be found in those lands.'

Joseph was amazed. The tin looked like it was of an exceptionally high quality, and it would fetch a fantastic price if he succeeded in his enterprise. It was a critical component for creating bronze, and fetched a far higher price than iron ever could. He had not expected to find such a valuable metal here. Fortune had favoured him this day.

Joseph negotiated an extremely agreeable price for as much tin as he could afford, saving only enough gold for their journey home. They agreed to meet Flavius the following day at noon, alongside the small island they had passed as they sailed into the channel. There, they would load the cargo on to Joseph's small boat and exchange the payment once it was safely aboard. If the winds were favourable, they would then continue on and make the journey across the Channel. After this, they would hop back along the Gaulish coastline, past Portugal and on to Israel, disguised as a poor fishing vessel. With a great deal of luck and no little skill, they hoped to avoid trouble and make it back to the port of Jaffa; in the meantime, though, it appeared they would have the opportunity to see a little more of this land before they departed its shores.

Joseph asked Flavius if there was any room available for them to stay at the fort for the night, and Flavius shook his head no.

'I am afraid not, Joseph. A century is returning from a scouting mission further inland today. All of the buildings and tents here will be taken over by them when they return, and they are a rough bunch, if truth be told. I would not have you or your boy suffer their company this night, but I have a private tent in a camp on the far side of the escarpment if you would like to use it for the evening?'

'If it will not inconvenience you, Flavius, we would be most honoured to accept your kind offer. It would also be a pleasure to explore some more of the land up here.'

'No problem for me,' he replied cheerfully, 'I can sleep anywhere these days. It's a useful trick to pick up in the army, and I mastered it long ago.'

Joseph and Jeshua gathered their belongings and followed Flavius back along the woodland path they had arrived from.

Crickets chirped noisily in the long grass and tiny birds sung their beautiful songs as they walked through wind-stunted woods along heather-lined paths. The late afternoon sun was hot on their faces and a cool, salty breeze floated up to them from the ocean below.

'Is the weather usually like this?' asked Joseph. 'It is a perfect day today.'

Flavius roared with uncontrollable laughter. 'I am sorry to laugh so, Joseph, but no, no, it most certainly is not. This land sees more rain than any I have ever known in my lifetime. It is absolutely remarkable how often it pours down here. Don't be deceived by the weather this last week; it can be extremely depressing during the long winter months. It must be what makes this land so green, though, and when the sun does shine, it transforms into one of the most beautiful places I have ever seen; but those days are too rare, unfortunately. When the weather turns foul, it is most unpleasant. The wind often blows like a tempest on the hilltop; the rain stings your face hard on those days. Hauling goods up and down the slopes is also very taxing for any who are stationed here. But on days like this, I must confess, it does feel special; there seems to be a sense of weightlessness up here.'

'And great age.' Jeshua offered.

Jeshua had been so quiet since they had first met that Flavius had begun to think the boy was a mute.

'You speak?' he jested, smiling at the young lad. 'Yes, great age too, young sir. The Regnii tribes occupied this site before we took it over, and it seems to have been an important place for them. There are enormous burial mounds up here. The legion dug one out when they arrived, and you would not believe what they found.' He paused for dramatic effect, and Jeshua and Joseph urged him to tell them.

'A chariot and a team of horses with a man still at the reins!'

'Incredible!' Joseph remarked.

'Looked like he had been there for a while too, as there was not much left of him, but that is an unusual burial custom to say the least, don't you think? The diggers found other things too,' he added excitedly. 'Golden treasures surpassing anything we have seen gifted to a dead man before. He must have been an important fellow in his time. We are thinking there must also be some rich gold mines in these lands somewhere, but we are yet to find them if indeed there are.'

Joseph and Jeshua both looked suitably impressed at the revelations, and Flavius continued walking in front until, a short while later, they came across a vast clearing filled with tents, soldiers and servants going about their daily routines. They could also see the beginnings of another fortification being constructed, on a high peak above the camp.

Flavius led them through the busy settlement and showed them the tent they would be utilising for the evening. It was beautifully furnished with rugs, cushions and an unlit brazier in the centre. They thanked him heartily, and Joseph offered him some coin for the trouble. Flavius assured them that he had already found a bunk for the night and that it was no trouble at all. Joseph was finding his trip to Albion to be most fortuitous, and everyone he had met so far was being extremely generous. It was not the sort of reception he was either used to or expecting, but sometimes you simply do meet good people, he acknowledged happily. Flavius waved them from the tent.

'Drop your carry bags here and come and join me for some food if you are hungry? I am certain it will be a fairly average stew of some sort, but it'll keep you going, and it's not done me any harm.'

They followed him back through the busy camp, taking in the scene around them. It was hard to imagine that all of these men were somehow functioning together, thought Joseph. While the organisation was hard to see at first, after a short while, the incredible cohesion became more apparent, and whilst not a supporter of bloodshed and conquest, Joseph had to admit that what these enormous groups of strong men had accomplished was utterly astonishing. Their well-structured armies and unity of purpose were quickly achieving ever more incredible feats of engineering across the world. Roman dominance was plain for all to see.

As they approached the camp kitchens, they became aware of raised voices and an ugly scene came in to view. Two soldiers were brutally kicking a slave on the ground, while many others stood around them and watched. The slave was bloodied and begging for his life, but the soldiers paid him no heed and continued with the merciless beating.

Flavius held up a hand and asked Joseph and Jeshua to wait where they stood while he dealt with the situation. Joseph nodded his head, and Jeshua and he watched and waited.

'What is going on here!' Flavius shouted as he approached. The men ceased their attack immediately. Joseph assumed that Flavius must have great influence within the camp, for the soldiers suddenly looked terrified.

'We caught him stealing food, sir!' the first soldier pleaded.

'Not for the first time either, I'd wager,' added the second, attempting to garner some just cause for his action, but unable to meet Flavius' eyes.

They fidgeted under his gaze, and Flavius knew there was more to this story than they were admitting. Their guilt and uneasiness were plain to see now they had been called to account.

'Camp protocol, is it not, sir?' asked the first soldier. 'We all swore an oath not to steal, including him, and we all know the punishment if we break it.'

'Silence!' commanded Flavius. 'This behaviour will not be tolerated, as well you know. It is not for you recruits to sentence a man to his punishment within this camp. We are not common thugs, we are soldiers of Rome, and we live by the rule of Rome. Or are you two grunts in charge now?' he bellowed.

They looked to the floor, becoming slowly aware that they had gone too far now that their rage was subsiding.

The bloodied slave was groaning in pain as he lay in the mud. His lip was split, his front teeth were missing and his right eye was a purple lump, swelling up fast. The small crowd of soldiers that surrounded them were looking childlike now, and Flavius addressed them all.

'So quick you are to judge and to take our law in to your own hands. It will not be tolerated, do you hear me?' he screamed. 'If a single man here has made no mistake in his life, let him continue the beating.' The crowd of soldiers began to recall their own shortcomings and their bloodlust was soon replaced by shame. More considered of their actions now, the men slowly dispersed and Flavius shooed them off with a contemptuous flick of his hand. He addressed the two accusers.

'You two men will take this wretch into your care and nurse him back to health with all of the kindness you can find within your miserable little souls. I will be watching you. If a hair more is harmed on this man's head, I will have you executed. Order must be maintained. You may rest assured that theft will not go unpunished, but we will follow Roman protocols and we will keep to Roman laws, not yours; do you understand?'

'Yes, sir!' they chimed, nodding their chastened agreement. Together, they picked up the fallen man and carried him off to the camp doctor.

Flavius waved Joseph and Jeshua over once the men had departed. 'Apologies for that ugly business, gentlemen. It is a difficult job managing these recruits. A rougher bunch of vagabonds I have never met, but truth to tell, these are exactly the sort of men you need to conquer nations.'

'We observed the encounter keenly,' said Joseph, 'and thought you handled the situation rather well. The men here clearly respect you, Flavius. Do you hold a high rank within the legion?' he asked, curious about Flavius' position.

'Yes Joseph, I am a tribunus angusticlavius, or a 'narrow-striped tribune'. My family hold much prestige within the senate. I work below the praefectus here. One of my duties is keeping the regular soldiers in order and making sure the camp is run correctly, but as you can see, it is not an easy job sometimes.' He shook his head, whimsically. 'Anyhow, now that vile incident is dealt with, let us eat, gentlemen!'

They sat down together on some short, three-legged stools and Flavius brought them some hot stew, served in carved wooden bowls. It was as promised; fairly bland, but filling and wholesome. They ate slowly, deeply grateful for the hot food, and talked more of the land and their hopes for the future as the sun dipped slowly away to the west once more. Joseph and Jeshua greatly enjoyed their last night in Albion in the company of Flavius. He had proven to be a most interesting man and an excellent contact for them to continue to do business with. Joseph and he would go on to become firm friends over the following years.

It had been a simple journey of trade and discovery, but one that they would never forget.

Epilogue…

Joseph and Jeshua travelled to many distant lands over the next twenty-six years. They spent some happy years in the lands of the Indus and made frequent trips to the pyramids in Egypt. Jeshua became fascinated by the enormous feats of construction there and longed to learn of their origins; but it seemed that nobody in the area knew of their history. 'They have always been there,' the local tribesmen had repeated, and no one knew their purpose. This seemed remarkable to Jeshua. He longed to know the meaning behind the mysterious structures.

They returned to Ipwinesfleet together on many occasions and soon ventured further along the coast to the tin mines in the lands of Cornwallium. Joseph and Jeshua had become men of the world and people often gathered together to hear their stories of far-off lands when they came into port. They had visited many countries and learned much; both had become talented storytellers.

Joseph of Arimathea
Year 33

Chapter - 2

〜〜〜〜

Joseph of Arimathea
Year 33

〜〜〜〜

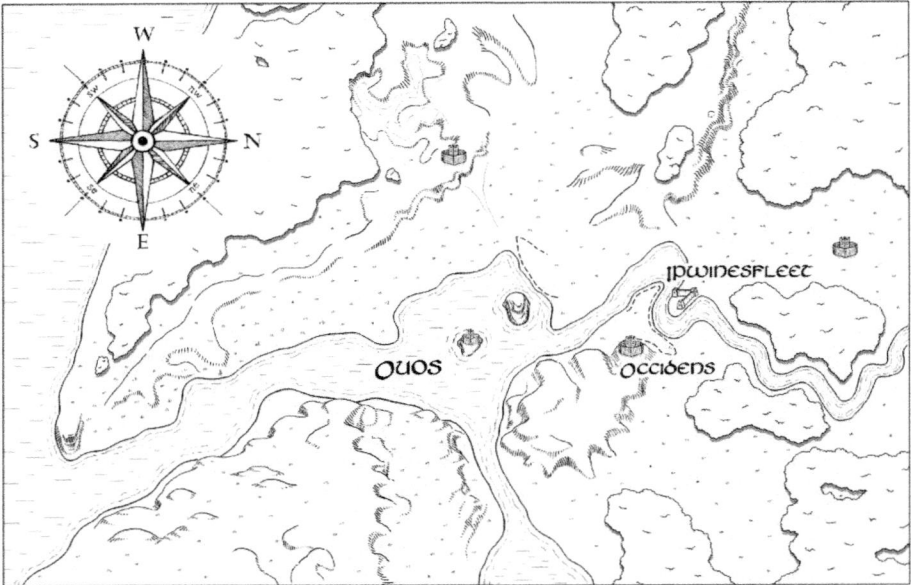

Joseph pulled in the mainsail and docked the small sailing boat at the familiar port of Ipwinesfleet. It had been a miserable journey. Paul, Simon, Andrew, Peter and he had spent the vast majority of the long trip in silence. They were still processing the events of the last months and were unable to forget the horrific images of the brutal torture inflicted on the man they had all loved so much. It was also hard to leave their brothers and their home behind; they would miss them dearly.

Jeshua had requested they undertake this journey to Albion while he had hung, suffering, on the cross; still attempting to spread wisdom into the world, even in his dying moments. They had obeyed his last wish, but none of them had wanted to go. To leave the land they loved so much was painful, but they trusted him, and had all done as he had instructed.

Joseph had become a very wealthy man in his lifetime, but he knew now that gold would never be enough; gold would not satisfy his heart. He felt hollowed out by witnessing the brutal torture and crucifixion of his son. How he had despised the people and the soldiers in Jerusalem leading up to that fateful day. Joseph had never been as disappointed in his fellow man as he had been over this last year. How easy the masses were to manipulate and deceive. How eager they were to cast blame. Such fearful and vindictive creatures. Jeshua had given his everything to help raise them out of ignorance and he had been rewarded with a cruel ending. The part of Joseph that believed in a fair world had died alongside Jeshua that day. It was clear to him now that there was terrible misfortune and sorrow to bear in one's life. This had proven to be a hard lesson for him. Through great suffering, his illusions had all been cruelly shattered, but this had not made him cold-hearted, neither had it led him to be hateful; somehow, he was now experiencing life from a new perspective, somewhat emptied of emotion, and it was strangely peaceful. Everything Joseph had considered to be real and vital up to that fateful day had now transformed into an illusion of his own making. He reflected that, somewhere along the way, he had not completely understood, or maybe accepted, that all possibilities could not exist without each other. It was a confusing concept to face.

Joseph had resigned his position as nobilis decurio before departing Israel. The thought of continuing work as the minister of mines in the Roman government no longer held any interest to him whatsoever. He could not, in good conscience, continue to work for the Empire that had murdered his only son. Jeshua had been outspoken and fearless, and had gained a large following. He had begun to wake up the masses, and this had threatened the power of the Roman Empire. They had responded with savage violence, and that was not an Empire Joseph could aid any longer. He had gathered a vast fortune in his position, and he would now attempt to put that wealth to good use in a new land, on the outer reaches of Roman-held territory. He would create his own community in the land of Albion, and attempt to teach humanity to evolve beyond murdering and manipulating their fellow man. He would teach them the ways of Jeshua.

A familiar figure appeared from the small stone dwelling of the harbourmaster.

'Mathias, how fares you?' asked Joseph as he neared, wondering why Eligius had not come to greet them.

'I am well, my friend.' They embraced warmly. 'And how are you, dear Joseph? You look changed.'

'Aye, Mathias, it has been a difficult time since I last saw you. Was it seven summers past now?' He pondered the time, and Mathias nodded his head in agreement. 'Where is Eligius? I have missed you both dearly.' Joseph looked back to the harbourmaster's dwelling once again, expecting him to appear at any moment.

'I am sorry to say that he passed away peacefully some months ago, Joseph. He spoke of you and Jeshua in his last days. I will take you to his burial mound on the high hill to pay your respects once you are settled.'

Tears formed in Joseph's eyes once again and he could not hold them back. The older he got, the more he lost, and though somewhat numbed to pain in recent months, the mounting hurt continued.

'That is sad news, Mathias, and I am sorry to say I have much of my own. I would dearly love to say my farewell, old friend, but first I must put my son to rest.' Joseph gestured with his hand, and Mathias looked down into the boat to see an emaciated body, wrapped neatly in white cloth. Shock and tears welled up from deep within Mathias' heart; he was stunned. It took him many minutes to gather his wits together, but after a while he wiped his tears away and embraced Joseph once again.

'Oh, Joseph. This is a sad meeting indeed. I am so sorry for your loss, my old friend. He was truly the finest of men. It saddens me greatly to know his light is now gone from this world. Please, you must let me help you lay him to rest, it would be my honour.'

Emotions ran high as together, and with great love and care, they lifted the body of Jeshua from the boat, then walked slowly up the hill toward the Roman mortuary tomb beneath the promontory. Joseph and Jeshua had purchased a chamber in this tomb on their last trip to Albion together and, for reasons known only to him, Jeshua had insisted he be interred here on his passing.

They descended the steps cut into the rise and arrived atop the wooden jetty. Turning here, they made their way along the low hillside, opened a small gate that led back to the tomb entrance, and entered the dark, silent crypt. Mathias lit a torch and located the chamber, hewn into the earth by the Romans here many decades ago, and in a quiet, peaceful recess, they laid Jeshua down gently, delivering him to his final resting place.

Joseph placed the spearhead that had pierced Jeshua's side atop his body, and next to his head he set the great golden cup Joseph had used to wash his son of blood, as he had requested. It was important, Jeshua had told him, though Joseph did not understand why. He rested his hand on Jeshua's chest and closed his eyes. 'No words are deserving enough for you, my son. I love you, and will see you again in better times, and in a better place.'

They all emerged from the mortuary tomb, crying tears of great sadness once again at the loss of their dear friend. Together, they slid the tombstone back into place, and left Jeshua behind for the final time, in the realm of the Manes.

Mathias pleaded for them to stay with him and they all gratefully agreed. He lit a fire and they sat late into the night, talking fondly of Jeshua and Eligius; reminiscing on better days and smiling at the memories. They ate some simple food and drank a little wine Mathias had been saving for a special occasion. They cried, they laughed, they remembered. It was good to be together that day.

Epilogue…

Over the next few weeks, Joseph and his friends began to construct a small church made of sturdy wicker hurdles above the tomb they had interred Jeshua in. It did not take long for many new apostles to join the ranks of Mathias, Paul, Simon and Joseph. These men were wise. These men were kind. They talked of the greater mysteries in life, and many began to listen. They helped to educate any who sought to learn. They taught great wisdom through parable. They talked about Jeshua and his life and spoke of his death and his bravery in the face of great misfortune. It was clear that people admired those qualities and, very quickly, courage and kindness in the face of adversity spread throughout the land.

Joseph put his money to good use, purchasing as much of the land in the surrounding areas as he could afford. He acquired farmland and vineyards, and together the apostles started to grow their own crops, and to produce their own wine. It was soon agreed that a small church would always be kept at the same location on the promontory at the port, but a larger church was now required; hundreds were joining their community, and a bigger space was needed for their gatherings. It was decided, therefore, that a new church would be erected near an old Roman encampment at the foot of Mutuantonis, close to the shoreline. The Romans had named this place Albion Street – it was the first road they had constructed when they landed on these shores, and it seemed appropriate to site it there. A cold spring fed a large pool nearby, and the icy water that flowed from it would serve them well in washing away the sins of man.

Joseph and Simon began to preach for mighty gatherings and many great men came to hear the teachings of Jeshua. Soon, the apostles also began the arduous process of converting those lessons into a written form, and it was not long before well-versed Christians taught in Albion - headed out into the world. Those great men began to preach the Christian lessons to any who would listen. A converted Roman general called George went south to Turkey, while Andrew went north to the lands of Caledonia. Joseph travelled west, to Glastonbury, which held a special place in his heart. Bartholomew went east, and others remained and tended well to their flocks in the south of Albion. Churches sprang up fast wherever those men travelled.

Soon, wealth began to flow into the church, and with it, greed and a lust for power crept slowly into the mind of Simon. None noticed his change in spirit until it was too late. Simon began to tarnish his soul as he delved deeply into the world of occultism,. Before the end of his life, he had become well known as 'Simon the Sorcerer'. He profited greatly from the church and distorted the true message of Jeshua to his own ends. He would leave a legacy of greed and vile behaviour behind in men who were supposed to know better, a legacy that would last for more than two thousand years.

Septimius Severus
Year 209

Chapter - 3

Septimius Severus
Year 209

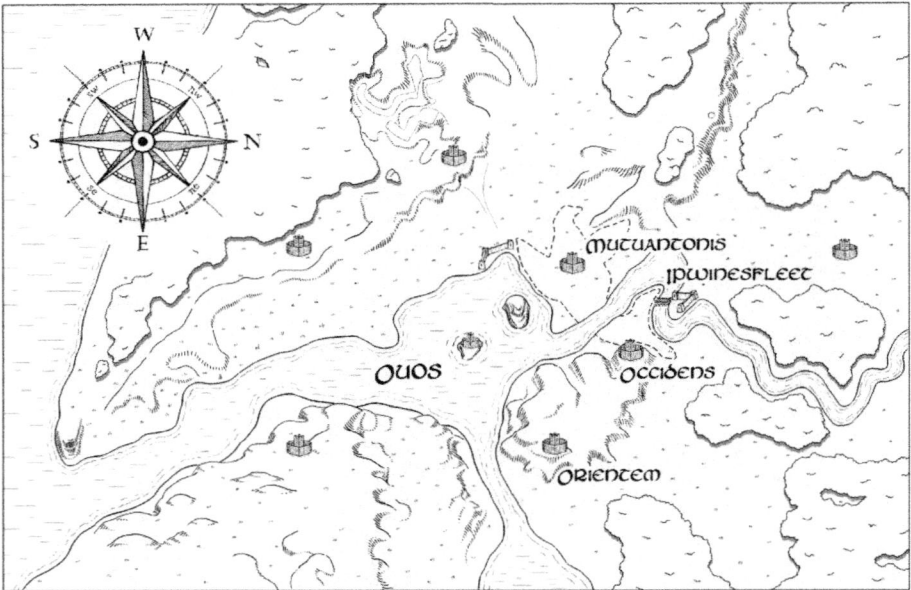

The fleet began to enter the Ouos valley. The first wave of the forty-thousand-strong army was arriving on the southern shores of Britain. The vast channel was filled with countless Roman triremes. Some had already landed along the valley slopes, and from there, troops had begun to file out from the boats, making their way to the various forts the Romans had constructed along the hilltops. All seven of these forts would be needed to house the greatest army the island of Britannia had ever seen arrive on its shores, and every single harbour space would be required to accommodate them. There was no single port large enough here to absorb so many men. Septimius shook his head in frustration. The logistics of moving this many soldiers – feeding them, housing them, arming them, and focusing them to his cause – was beginning to give him a headache, but he was a wise man and had prepared well for this enormous undertaking.

Caledonian wild men had risen up against the Romans in the north and Septimius was here to do what no other Emperor had managed so far; he was going to bring the entire island of Britannia under the heel of Roman law. They had taken the vast majority of the land already, but the Caledonians were using tactics the Romans seemed unable to defeat. Small bands of those untamed men would harass and attack the Roman lines as they proceeded into their lands, then dart back into the mountains with little loss to their numbers. There seemed to be no main overlord or king to bring to heel there, and it was becoming a real problem for them. To be thwarted so effectively by mere barbarians made Rome look weak.

With no obvious path to victory, Emperor Hadrian had left a clear border to divide the territories, splitting the country in two with an enormous wall that stretched for many miles across the current northern frontier of Britannia. It was a dangerous post that no soldier wished to be sent to, but the land of Caledonia would soon face the full might of the modern Roman legions, and Septimius was confident that the barbarians would be defeated this time.

He brought his mind back to the present, called for more wine, and considered his progress. Before he could even attempt to begin the daunting task of subduing the Caledonian barbarians, he had far more pressing issues to concern himself with. A large army needed focus and discipline; it needed a job to do or the men within it would grow idle. The food and wage costs of maintaining such a mighty force would then be wasted. Heavy labour kept the army strong while they waited to move further inland, so Septimius had set the men an impossible task; they were to build a permanent port wall and stone bridge, stretching from sea to sea, at the end of the tidal estuary. This would link Ipwinesfleet to the opposite shore, and create a secure bottleneck in the channel to protect the Roman citizens who had begun to settle along the riverbanks in great numbers further upstream.

The Romans had a firm foothold in Britannia now, having occupied the land for over two hundred years. They had succeeded in subjugating a significant portion of it, and it was from Dubris, Anderida, Mutuantonis and Ipwinesfleet that they had created the infrastructure they had needed to do this. Supply lines from Gaul were essential to the cause. Well-built, straight roads had also been constructed; the first of which was built from the port at Anderida west to the port at Ipwinesfleet, and the second from Ipwinesfleet to Londinium, once the south of the country had fallen entirely under Roman rule. Their mighty symbol of power on these shores, the town boundary shaped in the image of the Eagle of Rome, had also now been completed.

The extensive network of Roman roads in this land had cost many lives. Soldiers had been tasked to construct them but slaves had also been recruited; people who had not willingly and quickly submitted to Roman rule were captured and put to work. Many native inhabitants had died in the creation of their road network, and when they were in short supply, the army used the subjugated people as slaves whether they submitted to them, or not. The roads simply had to be built, and the lower the cost to Roman life, the better. The natives here were wild, untamed and uneducated in contrast to Rome's citizens, but they were also strong and made for excellent labourers. Many of them had strange red hair, pale skin and wild blue eyes; they were quite unlike the dark-skinned people of Septimius' homeland.

Septimius had been born in Libya and had begun his road to greatness in the family business, producing olive oil. It had made him an extremely wealthy man, and with this tremendous wealth he was able to gain status, with status he had gained influence, and then, after many years of war, he had gathered a vast army together in Vindobona 'Vienna' and seized Rome. As the new Emperor, he had then begun to travel his Empire, and during his unusually long reign of fifteen years, he had been required to quell only one rebellion. Albinus, a once-loyal supporter of Septimius, had risen up against him. Septimius had killed him at the Battle of Lugdunum. He had then beheaded Albinus, and sent that head to the Senate at Rome, delivering a clear message to any who would consider betraying him in the following years while he toured his Empire. He was now sixty-three years old and had become a mighty military leader, but he had one goal left to achieve before the end of his life. He had become intent on doing what no other Emperor had managed to accomplish; he would defeat the Caledonians and rule the entire island of Britannia. Septimius knew that if he accomplished this, he would never be forgotten.

Sitting in his campaign tent, set proudly atop the promontory of Ipwinesfleet, Septimius finished scratching his latest orders on to the papyrus scroll that would soon be sent to Rome. He had sited his tent next to an old, but well-kept wooden church and graveyard. Just beyond the church was a sunken bathhouse, constructed decades ago, and making use of one of the many hot springs cropping up in the lands surrounding Mutuantonis. He would not typically have chosen to site his sleeping quarters so close to a church, tombs and a graveyard, but there was really no choice in the matter – flat land on the promontory was in short supply. However, from here he could direct and oversee the construction of the bridge, and also make good use of the baths.

Tons of chalk and flint from the downland quarries to the east had now been mined and moved down to the opposite shore to construct the wall that would lead to the bridge. The chalk was being processed for turning into hydraulic lime to use in concrete and mortar. There seemed to be a constant fog of the white dust floating in the air these days, and that dry air was not good for the men's lungs. Those working closest to the lime had their faces covered with wetted cloths in an attempt to reduce the amount of dust entering their airways, but it was mostly in vain; they all had dry hacking coughs at the end of each day, and those poor workers often died younger than others.

Another critical component to a successful campaign, Septimius knew, was hygiene. Latrines and washing facilities were becoming very important right now; disease could be spread rapidly if the waste from forty thousand troops was not effectively managed. Septimius did not want to be exposed to it in his weakened state, so he had decided that his headquarters' lavish bathhouse would be for his use only. He did not want to invite infection from the filth coming off his soldiers as they bathed, and he found the hot waters of the baths eased the pain in his aching bones considerably. Septimius was most unwilling to let his men witness his frailty, so late at night, and with guards posted outside the building, he would slip into that soothing water, easing away the aches and stresses of the day. It was his favourite time; a momentary respite from decision-making and the ceaseless questioning from his Praetorians. He knew it was a luxury he was coming to rely on, but soon he would have to leave this place behind as he and his army began the long march north. He shuddered again at the thought of the long sea voyage ahead, and of being bounced along the roads in his litter for hundreds of miles; it filled him with dread. He knew he was too old for this life now, but what choice did he have, he asked himself. His son was not the man he had hoped he would be, not the leader that Rome needed to rule the Empire. He was weak and conniving, and Septimius knew that he himself was to blame for this. He had spoiled him and made him weak.

It had not escaped his attention in his long life that it was those that struggled, suffered and fought for what they had that became the people who gained fortitude, reliability and steadfastness. Too often now he had witnessed the sons of great men become whining, entitled weaklings, mostly interested in squabbling and boasting. Having never struggled for anything in life, they had become worthless beings who could not be relied upon in a crisis, and yet, to his dismay, these were the men who now filled the Senate and controlled the populace. He shook his head in disgust. He had brought another weak man into this world, and he hated himself for it. However, in an attempt to correct this error he had ordered his son, Caracalla, to come with him to Britannia to see if he could become the man that Rome needed him to be before Septimius' life ran out. It seemed a wasted effort. Caracalla was missing; no doubt in the local taverns, drinking and whoring. Septimius shook his head again, but ruefully forced a smile. Maybe his son had the right idea. War was becoming tedious in the extreme, but the Roman army was a machine that could not be stopped, and it had fallen upon Septimius to keep that machine focused to the cause of Rome.

He set down his quill. 'Enough with this self-pity,' he said to himself as he got up from his chair. His hand-servants quickly moved towards him, clasped his purple robe to his shoulder hasps, and handed him his golden, red-plumed helmet. Septimius placed it on his head, then stepped purposefully from the tent into a cacophony of noise as soldiers swarmed the lands around him like ants set to task.

As he took stock of his surroundings, he noticed that a small congregation of Christians had assembled by the old church nearby. They were cheerfully embracing each other, presumably before entering for prayer, he thought. The Christians were a strange lot, he thought; like another species of human, all bent on love and peace in a war-stricken world. He could not fathom how the religion had survived in such a dangerous place. He had only lived a life of war, and they seemed alien to him; alien and weak, he mused. However, the Emperors of the past had discovered long ago that the easiest and fastest way of conquering nations then profiting quickly from them was to absorb them in just as they were found. They would then be slowly lulled into the lifestyle, and consequently the will, of Rome. In as little as one generation, the people had usually forgotten who they once were, but not the damn Christians, it would seem, and strangely, with freedom of choice, many Roman citizens had also now converted to Christianity. Septimius could not understand it. He drew his attention from them, and set off toward the docks.

It was nearing midday. The sun was high, and a cool, refreshing breeze was coming in from the south as he neared the wharf. Septimius noticed that one of his mighty cargo ships had made port. Men were scurrying around the decks, hard at work, as gigantic crates and cages were unloaded. The guards at the harbourside saluted sharply as Septimius approached the steps that led to the wooden walkway. Septimius ignored them.

'Careful with that crate, soldier!' cried the harbourmaster. 'Don't get too close to it, or you may lose a hand!'

'Yes, sir!' the young soldier on the boat replied smartly, knowing full well what the crate contained, and more than happy to oblige in staying well away from it.

A great roar sounded suddenly from within the box, and the young soldier stumbled backwards from the incredible volume of it, a terror gripping at his heart from the sheer displeasure sounding from the enormous lion contained within. He knew that if the beast got out, it would tear him apart in a matter of seconds. He had witnessed it on many occasions in the arenas, and it was certainly not how he wanted to die. The harbourmaster laughed at him and the lad reddened at his obvious display of fear, before noticing with stunned terror that the Emperor himself was watching him coldly.

Septimius strode down the solid oak steps to the wooden walkway, unamused by the scene.

'How goes the intake, harbourmaster?' he enquired flatly.

The harbourmaster saluted, and braced himself for a dressing-down; Septimius did not like foolery. 'We are just finishing unloading the beasts, Emperor.' He could not withstand Septimius' withering stare, and looked to the floor at his feet. 'The gladiators are all under lock and key, and the fleet will soon be ready to set sail back to Gaul for reloading.'

'Very good,' Severus replied shortly. He was about to berate the young lad on the ship for his cowardice, but his attention was then drawn to an enormous crate, directly behind the boy, containing the impressive lizards that he had acquired many years ago in Africa Proconsularis. They had come to him along the Silk Road from Indonesia, and were now his most prized possessions. They had better have survived the journey unscathed, he thought, or there would be hell to pay. Still yet to be fully grown, there were three of them, all around five feet in length, and hard to tell apart for an untrained eye, but he knew each by name. He had initially purchased them with the intention of setting them against gladiators and other mighty beasts in the arena, but he had quickly changed his mind and grown fond of the strange creatures.

'How fared my serpents on the voyage, Captain?' Septimius asked, as a grizzled Roman seaman appeared from below decks.

The captain turned as he rose from the bowels of the ship, momentarily surprised at the Emperor's unexpected presence on the wharf, but he quickly regained his composure, acknowledged the Emperor with a sharp salute, and then addressed him confidently.

'They kicked up a mighty fuss as we set sail, but soon settled down once we were underway, Emperor. The lad that was bitten whilst loading them died on the voyage over, however; in great pain from the bite he received, he was. Screaming so much that he wet himself. He was driving us to distraction with his convulsions, so I sent him on his way, as was the kind thing to do.'

The captain sounded dangerously close to complaining, thought Septimius. He raised an eyebrow at his tone. 'They are a dangerous creature, as I had previously warned you, Captain. You must never underestimate the power of an imprisoned beast, and especially not a poisonous one!'

'Yes, Emperor,' the captain replied. 'He was a foolish lad, but it was a cruel passing, to be sure.'

Septimius cared little; it was just another death among thousands left in his wake. 'Yes, it is a great shame,' he said flippantly. 'Get my serpents housed. Site them next to the bathhouse – they will prefer the warmer temperatures provided by the hot waters there. I intend to convert it in to a habitation for them before the seasons change. This place is a cold hell in winter, Captain, and I fear it is not far off now. Inform me when the fleet is ready to set sail back to Gaul. I must talk with the overseer constructing the bridge.'

'Yes, sir!' the captain replied smartly.

The captain, the harbourmaster and the crew bowed their heads swiftly in respect as Septimius and his honour guard departed. They all blew a sigh of relief once he was out of earshot – Septimius was an unpredictable man.

Septimius continued to make his way along the wharf with his personal guard following close behind. Where the estuary curved sharply around a tight bend and then flowed on around the promontory, the construction of many mighty stone arches was now well underway. Those colossal feats of blockwork were needed to support the enormous weight of the bridge that would span the gap across the sea channel and link the two shores. The bridge would also create an impenetrable bottleneck that would be used to make the lands beyond, safe from attacking marauders.

The overseer had seen Septimius coming, and had prepared himself well for his latest verbal assault.

'Progress seems slow this last week, Titus,' Septimius stated accusingly as he approached.

'We are going as fast as we can, Emperor. Everything is running more efficiently now the sandstone blocks are arriving with more regularity.'

'Trouble with the quarry-masters, Titus? We can find new men if they are proving incompetent. Men we have, Titus – time we do not. We must accelerate the build immediately. We have been stuck here for too long already!'

'Your will, Emperor,' Titus replied, bottling up an anger he would not dare let his face express.

'And the walls?' Septimius added.

'The walls and fortifications are well underway, Emperor. I believe we are now working at an optimal rate.'

'We need better than optimal, Titus,' Septimius sniped. 'If you cannot speed this operation up, I will find somebody who can.'

'I will do all that I can to improve our work output, Emperor,' responded Titus calmly.

Septimius nodded his head, sneered, and with nothing left to criticize, continued along the wharf to further inspect the construction work. Titus watched Septimius as he departed, wondering what it would feel like to shove a knife through the Emperor's heart, and the expression he might make as he came to understand what had just happened. He smiled meekly at the departing soldiers, and returned to his work.

Epilogue…

With an iron fist, Septimius completed the bridge's construction and linked the shores at the far end of the Ouos estuary, firmly establishing control of the surrounding lands. He vastly improved the fortifications in the area, and created safe shipping routes from Gaul to Albion. When he departed Ipwinesfleet, he gave over the bathhouse to his serpents. It was converted into a temple according to his instructions. The walkway was lit with burning ewers, and blood sacrifices were regularly made to the beasts. As time passed by, one of the three serpents Septimius had brought to those shores laid a clutch of twenty-one eggs. Many of those lizards died young, some were sold to wealthy landowners in the locality, and others escaped and found their way to many of the hot springs located all over the downs of Sussex. These springs soon became known as 'Knucker Holes'.

Only a handful of Romans knew what the strange serpents were, but none of the local inhabitants had ever seen anything like them. One of the few species capable of asexual reproduction, they continued to survive in those lands for close to a thousand years. The dragon legends of Sussex were born, and two centuries of Roman dominance in Britannia followed, but it was not to last.

Mutuantonis had become a well-established town and Ipwinesfleet a flourishing port before Septimius headed north to conquer the Caledonians, but even with his mighty army and Roman dominance in warfare, he did not succeed. The legions that entered that territory were never seen again.

Caracalla could not live up to his father's expectations, and unwilling to live life under his heel, he attempted to murder Septimius on their journey north and to usurp the throne from him, but he was weak and his father was strong. When the moment came, he could not go through with it. Septimius died of natural causes at Eboracum 'York' in the year 211. Caracalla took control of the Empire with his brother Geta, but Caracalla was not a man who wished to share rulership. He had his brother murdered by the Praetorian Guard and took total control. He was a cruel and tyrannical leader, quickly quelling dissent with brutal, bloody violence.

During Caracalla's reign, Germanic forces began to attack the southern shores of Albion once more, so he returned to Ipwinesfleet for a short while, assuming his role as King of the Britons to keep the land firmly under the control of the Roman Empire. He travelled far, created the mighty Baths of Caracalla in Rome and introduced a new currency to the Empire, but as was common among leaders of Rome, he was eventually assassinated by one of his own soldiers in the Praetorian Guard. He was hated by his people and they were glad his time was over.

Magnus Maximus
Year 383

Chapter - 4

Magnus Maximus
Year 383

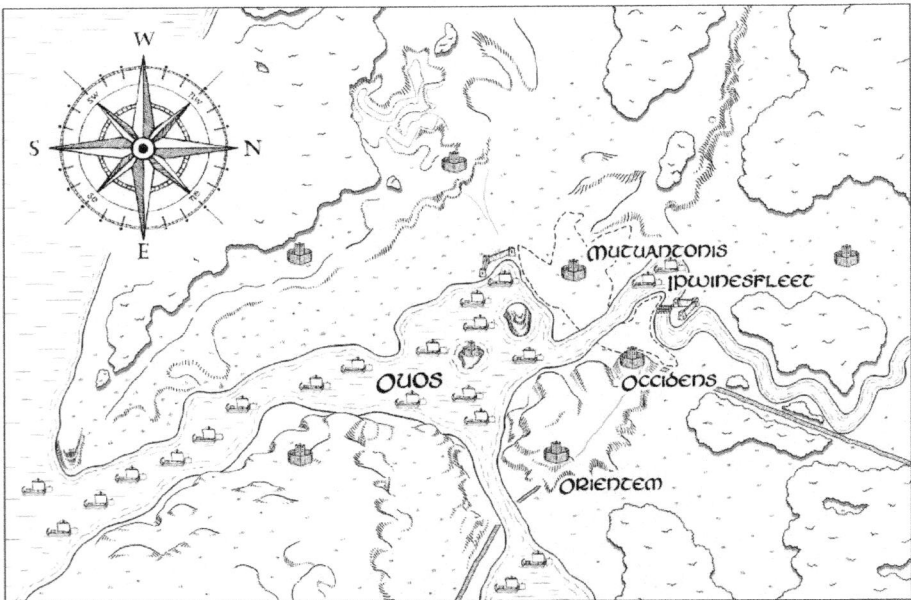

'Emperor Constantine has ordered our return to Rome, Praefectus – we must do as he instructs or the Empire will crumble. We can come back to Britannia and reclaim the land in the years to come, but if we do not aid Rome now, all will be lost!'

Maximus paced restlessly on the ramparts as the Praefectus brought problem after miserable problem to him. He looked down on the chaotic scene below him from his high vantage point on the great hill to the east of Ipwinesfleet. Citizens of Britannia from the entire country were flooding into the port, desperate to board any ship they could find room on, and to follow the soldiers out of the country. With no army left to defend them, it would only be a matter of time before the bloodshed began here. The Roman populace had enslaved and grown wealthy off the backs of the local inhabitants, and they had not forgotten that affront to their liberty, even centuries later.

Thirty years had now passed since the Roman garrisons at Hadrian's Wall had abandoned their posts in a fateful act of rebellion. From that day onwards, the Picts and Scots had ravaged the land and taken fierce revenge on their would-be conquerors. Maximus had been fighting this losing battle for many long, depressing years. In a cruel reversal of fortune, his people were now being slaughtered, raped, and taken into slavery. Carts filled with their most valuable belongings were crammed along the road. The army was struggling to contain the panic and manage the situation. The Roman citizens were furious. They were all being forced to abandon their homes, or face living in the country undefended, and to add insult to injury, they were now being told that they could not take their possessions with them; there was simply not enough room on the ships. The choice was made simple for them: either they stayed with their belongings and took their chances here, or they boarded a boat and left without them. The Romano Britons were being made to choose fast, and those at the front of the lines were swiftly sorting through their belongings to take the most valuable items they could find and hide on their persons. Coins and jewels were the most obvious choices for all, and some of the wealthier women now looked utterly ridiculous as they attempted to put on all of the precious items they owned at the same time. This obscene display of wealth was now making the divide between rich and poor so evident that the Roman citizens were fighting amongst themselves once they had won their place on a boat. Maximus watched as another outraged lady of Rome became embroiled in a bitter disagreement. As her seething outburst reached a righteous crescendo, it seemed her would-be victim had heard enough of her shrill complaints. He reached forward, clasped a hand over her mouth, then pushed her overboard in all of her finery. The weight of her wealth dropped her to the seabed like a stone and she drowned quickly, with no chance of rescue even in the shallow waters of the harbour. No one attempted to aid her.

He saw that some of the larger boats were now beginning to set sail for Gaul, while further out in the channel, other boats were on their way back to help ferry the tens of thousands of people thronging into Ipwinesfleet to escape the madness. Teams of soldiers by the port were now gathering up and sorting through the possessions that had been left behind; piling up the abandoned wealth of the Romano-Britons and then burning the carts and anything left over that was flammable to create room for the next wave of refugees. A pillar of black smoke had been making its way to the heavens for many days now and the roads were blocked with carts. There was not a breath of wind, and it was hot, unbearably hot. It was like the country itself was punishing their arrogance as they departed.

Maximus waved over his general. 'We must keep order, general. From this moment forward, treat any riotous behaviour with a brutal response; execute a few of the louder troublemakers if you have to. The crowds are close to overwhelming our forces and if they begin to surge, there will be no stopping them. Better to terrify them into submission than for all of our chances of escape to be destroyed. Do it now!'

'Yes sir,' the general replied. He saluted sharply, then turned and hurried off urgently to fulfil his task.

Maximus wiped the sweat from his face as he looked across the valley to the north. His mind returned once again to the Roman citizens of Britannia who had decided to remain here. Some of the landowners who were wealthy enough to maintain their own private armies were hoping, it seemed, for a continuation of their lifestyle. They were simply unwilling to abandon the lives they had created here and it was understandable, he thought – their families had lived here for generations. It was the only life they knew, but it was a decision they would likely come to regret. Maximus had seen the savagery of the warrior tribes in the country to the north, and the marauding Swedes and Danes would also soon hear of the Roman departure. He had little doubt that they would come in force to seize the land, and he knew, deep in his heart, that the Romano-Britons would not last long without the protection of the Roman army. He shuddered at the horrors he knew were to come for them, but for the time being he had other issues to contend with. Namely, what to do with the pile of hoarded treasure which was now growing obscenely large as the Roman citizens abandoned their belongings.

It was truly remarkable how much wealth these people had obtained. So many fine items were being left behind, it boggled the mind. Maximus thought it interesting how willing these people were to abandon that wealth when the threat of war was upon them. He had known that threat like few others, and because of this, he knew that real wealth came from your perceptions and your actions in this life, they did not come from what you gathered while you were here, but it did not seem like these people were anywhere near understanding this concept. He watched as another fight broke out by the docks. As was always the way in life, lies were now becoming exposed, and people were beginning to show their true colours. They were an ugly lot for the most part, and whether they knew it or not, he thought sadly, they would likely get what they had earned.

Maximus' critical eyes scoured the scene below, and his gaze fell on the old serpent temple, dug neatly into the earth of the promontory to tap the hot springs located beneath. It was a beautiful construction, but was also perhaps the ideal place to begin storing this accumulated wealth. There was simply no way the army could take all that had been abandoned with them, and time was of the essence. They would not be able to travel to Condate Riedonum with all those items weighing them down as they marched through Gaul. Perhaps the temple could be repurposed as an underground vault, he mused. The heavy labour of digging into the earth and building a solid roof had already been accomplished, and the lizards that continued to live there would also be a very effective deterrent. Maximus called over another officer.

'Praetorian, order your men to task. Begin splitting that abandoned wealth into two piles – small items in one pile, and larger items in the other. Any thievery will be punished severely, but assure the soldiers they will be paid! We will take what we can reasonably carry with us through Gaul, and leave the larger items and anything excess to our needs to collect on our return. If we are to have any hope of retaking Britannia, we will need that wealth to accomplish the task, so we must hide it. It is becoming apparent that we will need a vast space to house it all safely, so begin stacking the larger items on the walkway surrounding the temple. Do not get too close to the serpents – their bite is poisonous and they have a taste for human blood, but their eyesight is poor. They will often leave the pool to bask in the warmth of the sun during the daylight hours. Do not take unnecessary risks around them. Load the items only when the beasts have left the enclosure, and make sure they have been well fed. When all has been placed there, we will cover the entire structure with earth until no trace of the place remains, and the promontory looks only like the mound it once was. You will leave one low access point open from the temple to the estuary for the beasts' survival, but conceal it. It would also be wise for us to fill in the old mortuary tomb entrance further up the slope so that no robbers are tempted to go poking around there in the future. An honour guard will be left to protect those treasures, and they will wait here for our return. I will leave it to you to decide which men you would choose to undertake this task. They should be led by the most trustworthy of your captains, lest greed overcomes them, and they will be ordered to speak not a word of what is beneath their feet until Rome returns to these shores or the memory of what took place here dies with those that witnessed it.'

'Your will, Emperor,' replied the praetorian. He saluted smartly, turned, and headed off in search of his officers to begin this daunting new task set before him. Emperors had a mighty knack of ordering the impossible and then expecting it to somehow be accomplished yesterday, he thought. Somebody had to actually do the work, and, come hell or high water, just as he always did, the praetorian would get it done.

⁕

Maximus awoke with a start. He had not meant to fall asleep with so much to do, but after three days and two nights of problem-solving, his mind had finally rebelled and sleep had taken him. His head was fuzzy from heavy dreams and the stress of endless decision-making. He stood and splashed his face from the silver washing bowl his slaves had arranged for him. He splashed some more on his neck and scrubbed his face, hands and arms, before drying himself vigorously with a coarse towel. He almost felt human now, he thought to himself. He stretched his back and cracked his fingers.

Stepping from his tent, he crossed the courtyard, climbed the ladder to the lookout tower, and saw the situation had not improved much while he had slept. The roads were still packed with carts and refugees as far as his eyes could see. The fires still burned and the people were still very disgruntled, but the situation was under control. At least for now. It seemed that the three crucified men, clearly displayed on the hillside, had successfully cowed the masses who, despite the squalid conditions they endured as they waited for a place on a boat, were now containing the collective fear of being left behind, and were behaving far more sensibly.

Across the bay, he saw that his soldiers had begun the enormous undertaking of loading the abandoned goods into the bathhouse. Hundreds of men were moving tons of chalk and flint to block up the entrance to the mortuary tomb. Stonemasons were reinforcing the vaulted ceiling over the hot baths, and a tremendous amount of dirt was being moved there to cover the entire structure once the work was completed.

Boats were still making their way to and from Gaul, transporting the citizens to safer lands under firm Roman control, but the Scots and Picts were working their way south quickly, and reports of mass slaughter in nearby lands were coming in daily. It was becoming urgent now. At the current rate of progress, it seemed that not all of these people were going to make it. The might of Rome was crumbling before his very eyes.

Maximus longed to leave this chaotic place and return to lands where Roman authority would not be questioned, but even there now the citizens of Rome who had been evacuated from places like this would not forget the defeat they had suffered. News of the decline in Roman dominance would spread far and wide across the Channel. They were on the run, and once the rest of the Empire smelled blood, they too would turn on their captors. The sheer level of ineptitude and blatant corruption in the Senate at Rome had weakened the state and stretched its resources to breaking point, and now that Rome was being attacked by the ruthless Hun, there seemed little hope of preserving their mighty rule.

Epilogue...

During the following century, the Roman Empire began to crumble. The legions never returned to the shores of Britannia, but the remaining citizens and soldiers who had refused to depart their homeland eventually banded together in the lands surrounding Mutuantonis and took control of the many forts in the area. The port of Ipwinesfleet and the great fort atop the high hill remained under the stable control of experienced veterans in the Roman army. They protected the people there, and held fast the secret of the hoards of treasure beneath the promontory, but one by one, the original guard of Roman soldiers grew old and passed away, until only one lone man remained who remembered what had occurred there. It was many years later that he finally left the world, the last member of a once-mighty fighting force, lamenting his loneliness. The secret hiding place was lost to the world for three hundred and thirty-four winters, and the serpent temple and the tomb of Jeshua were left hidden, side by side, silently waiting for their discovery.

The Romano-Britons in the surrounding lands fared well for a short while in the army's absence, but for the most part, the people turned from fighting and adapted to farming over the following century. True warriors left among them were few and far between. They did not fare well when Germanic tribes began to raid the land with ferocious regularity.

Aelle
Year 477

Chapter - 5

Aelle
Year 477

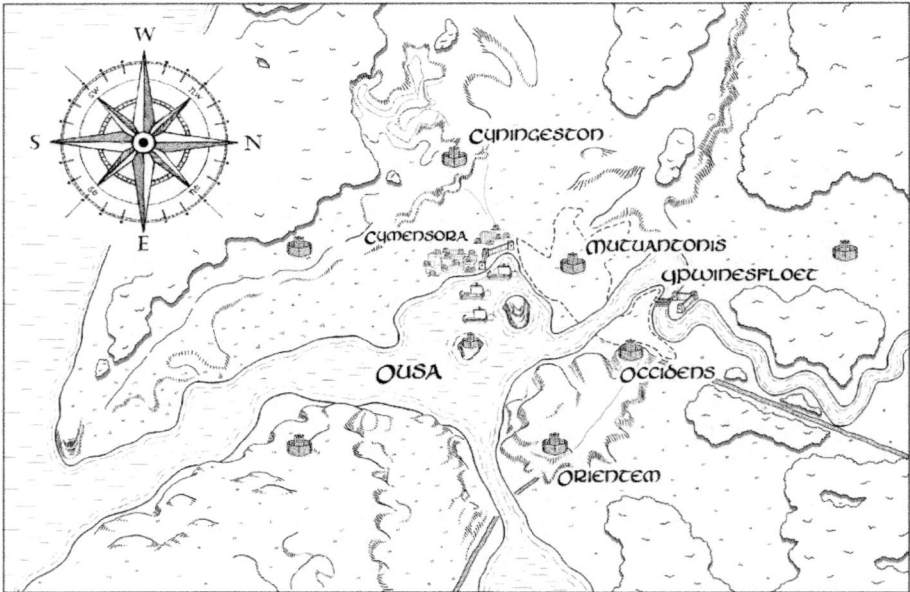

The small fleet of Saxon ships entered the Ousa estuary. There was not a breath of wind, and the hill fog was thick around them, concealing their presence in the hours before dawn.

'Drop the sails,' ordered Aelle quietly. 'They are no use to us now. Oars only!'

The crews did as instructed, then retook took their places on the wooden benches to row the longships in for the final stretch of their journey. Their oars dipped and pulled quietly as they glided into the valley. The crews could see no warning beacons, and it seemed their presence had so far gone undetected. The Saxons had waited for many long and dreary weeks in a small bay further along the coast for these conditions, and now the thick fog had finally arrived, the time was upon them.

'We will make land soon,' whispered Aelle. 'Be ready!' His eyes were wide, and his blood began to surge strongly through his veins as the threat of battle approached.

The Saxon warriors tightened their belts and mail straps, unsheathed their seax swords and their short-handled hammer axes, then began to stretch their limbs, readying for the carnage ahead. The time had come; they must win or die. Hunger was gripping their people. Their homeland was harsh and infertile. Food shortages were becoming common among the populace, and if they did not find richer lands to farm and hunt in, they would all perish in the terrible grip of starvation. That was not a fate they wished for themselves, or for their kinsmen. The mighty hill fort of Cyningeston would give them everything they needed to take control of these lands and save their people, but first they had to win it.

The lead ship struck the shore, and soon after, the two other vessels beached alongside. Quickly and quietly, the warriors leapt from the first boat and gathered together. The bowmen and the warriors from the other ships joined their ranks soon after. None of them made a sound. If they were to succeed in this mission, stealth and cunning would have to be their allies. They had chosen their night well – Aelle could barely see beyond his arm's reach in the cloying fog.

They moved together as one, a dread war-band intent on victory or death, and crept silently towards the port at Cymensora. The shore at the head of the eagle was silent. Waves lapped gently at the wharf and their boots crunched softly into the wet shingle along the edge of the estuary. The small village at the foot of the great wooden hill fort would be caught sleeping, and in addition to the fog, this was the second advantage the Saxons had.

Aelle halted their approach and signalled three of his warriors forward. He pointed at the shadowy building in front of them, slid his finger across his neck and then held it to his lips. They nodded their understanding and crept forward together, drawing their knives. Ever so slowly, they eased up the latch on the door. It creaked a breath as they pushed it forward and they froze in place, their ears tuning into the silence for any signs of alarm, but when nothing came, they slid quietly inside.

Aelle heard simultaneous, muffled grunts as the assassins dispatched the sleeping men within. The warriors exited the building cold-faced, and the war-band moved on. Wraithlike they went from building to building, quietly executing as many of the enemy as they could manage before their presence was detected and the alarm was raised.

Aelle and his twenty-one best men, quickly moved ahead of the rearguard, following the narrow path through the impenetrable mists towards the hilltop. He could sense their luck was about to run out. It had been easy so far, and that was a good sign for them, but he knew it could not last. He cursed himself silently; almost as soon as he had finished the thought, an ear-piercing scream rang out in the windless night. Aelle and his men were already halfway up the steep rise to the fort when the cry sounded, and now they surged on as fast as their limbs could carry them. They could barely see each other through the thick fog as they ascended the muddy slope. It was brutally hard going, and their pace slowed alarmingly as they slid and scraped their way up the steep incline, but the Saxon warriors were almost there, and it seemed the gates to the fort had still not been opened. The Romano-Britons had been slow in gathering themselves inside the defensive structure. Finally, though, the warning bells from inside the fort rang out into the night as the war-band crept up to the wall and crouched low in the fog and the black shadows of the night, but the Britons were too late.

The war-bands Aelle had left behind in the village were now setting fires and causing noisy, bloody slaughter in the impenetrable mists below. He had hoped this would lure the mounted Britons out of the fort, and once they had charged down the hillside, the Saxons could then pile inside, shut the gates behind them and dispatch the remaining footmen. It was an audacious plan, but they were fierce warriors and it was their best hope. If they failed now they would all die, and so much could still go wrong. Aelle turned his mind to the moments ahead.

The heavy gates to the fort creaked opened and, as Aelle had foreseen, the mounted Britons charged straight through and down the steep slope, unaware of the danger lurking outside their door. He held his men back, waiting for a heartbeat more, and sure enough, he heard the urgent march of foot-soldiers as they followed after the mounted knights. The Saxon warriors had set many raging fires below, and the cries for aid from the inhabitants there caused the soldiers to surge on down the slope. The hilltop went quiet as they disappeared into the mists, and then Aelle heard the great gates begin to swing shut. He waved his men forward urgently now, charging at the gates without a sound, and his warriors followed him in step.

The gate-men did not know what had hit them. Aelle's hammer axe embedded itself in the first guard's skull, and the man to his right dispatched the second guard with a swift lunge of his sword. The guard dropped to his knees in total shock as the blade pierced his neck and exited through his spine. He slumped soundlessly to the ground with a look of deep confusion on his face as a muddy boot pushed into his chest and the blade was swiftly withdrawn. Without a single cry, the twenty-one warriors set to their bloody work. Half the remaining Britons were down before they even knew what was happening, and the Saxons had now barred the gates from the inside; there would be no escape. The parapets and lookout towers were quickly being overtaken, and soon the numbers were in the Saxons' favour.

It seemed like mere heartbeats had passed before the fort was largely under their control. The few remaining soldiers and inhabitants, who had finally understood what was happening to them, were now banding together by the rear wall and it seemed they were attempting to form a shield wall that could cost many lives if the Saxons attacked it head on. Aelle had heard of this old defensive strategy for which the Roman army had been famous, and he ordered his men to keep clear of them and not to advance. He called out to the enemy in the Latin tongue as the first light of dawn grew slowly in the east, and the blurred shadows of the soldiers appeared in the stifling mists.

'You have lost and you are surrounded!' he bellowed. 'Throw down your arms and we will let you live. If you refuse, I will order my men on the parapets to cover you with buckets of pitch and we will burn you alive. The choice is yours. You have ten heartbeats to decide.' As he knew it would, the silence lasted only a moment before the sound of dropping weaponry and shields echoed over to him.

'Bind the prisoners, gag them and keep them safe. We will need information. One of those men is sure to be the overlord of this fort, so do not kill them, or by Woden, I will take your lives!'

The Saxons set to work, and in minutes the prisoners were secured, the buildings inside the fortification had been checked and cleared, and with one more push, they would win their salvation. Fortune had favoured them; the grain stores were full.

Aelle instructed his men to follow him to the walls above the gate. They did not have to wait there for long. The light of dawn was quickly burning away the eerie mists below and the mounted Britons, confused at the lack of invaders they had encountered in the village, could now be heard as they made their way back up the steep slope to the fort. They had witnessed many horrors and found few survivors while they had searched the buildings, but, even more alarmingly, no enemy had been found. It had appeared to them like demons had murdered their people. They were confused and terrified, seeking the sanctuary of home, but that was not to be their fate.

The lead horseman called up to the tower as they filed up the hill. 'Open the gates!' he cried, but was met only with stony silence. Others joined him, and they began to crowd together as they waited outside the wall. They were tired, and a horrible uneasiness was building inside them.

'Open the gates!' cried the lead horseman desperately once more, but was met again with total silence. He then began to pick out the figures of armed men on the walls and screamed at them, terror beginning to cut through his voice, 'Why do you not answer me?'

And then his confusion cleared, as with widening eyes, he finally recognised the Saxon warriors on the parapets, and as a hail of arrows rained down upon him from close quarters and from every direction.

Down in the village, as the horsemen had arrived, the Saxon rearguard had slipped away quietly into the dark mists and made their way in silence up the hillside to flank the returning men. They had then lain camouflaged and low, hiding in the black shadows of the night, but within bow-shot range of the front gate. The closely packed and terrified Britons were slaughtered in minutes once the enemy arrows were let loose, and the Saxons won Cyningeston from the Britons with little loss to their numbers.

Aelle left the men outside the walls to strip the corpses of valuables and to butcher the horses for meat. He ordered the gates to be opened for his men once their work was done, and set off to interrogate the prisoners. They were a miserable-looking lot in the light of day. Clearly, these men were not the Roman soldiers of old. They seemed weak, and were obviously terrified of the Saxon men that held them.

Aelle was an intelligent man, and had spent many years learning the language of the Romans in his homeland from captured slaves. He was not yet fluent, but his understanding of the tongue was proficient enough to communicate clearly.

'Which of you is the overlord here?' he asked. The prisoners seemed confused at his knowledge of their language but remained silent, staring at the ground, and they did not answer.

'Look at me and tell me which of you is the leader here or, so help me, I will butcher you all where you kneel!'

The captives raised their heads, and Aelle caught the flicker of two of the soldiers' eyes as they looked to their lord for instruction. The man they had given away remained silent. Aelle grabbed him by the shirt and pulled him face down into the muddy puddle by his feet, then placed his boot on the back of the man's head.

'Is this your lord?' he asked the prisoners again as the man beneath his heel began kicking and clawing for breath. The soldiers were silent still.

'I would wager you only have moments before this man drowns beneath my boot, and if he dies, I will execute you all, so if you want to live, then answer me right now!'

'He is the Vortigern! By God, let us live, it is he!' cried one of the terrified Britons, pointing to the man beneath Aelle's boot.

Aelle nodded to his guard, and the warrior cut open the traitor's throat from ear to ear. His hands clawed uselessly at the warm life pouring down his chest, and as the man's body slumped into the mud, Aelle released his boot from the overlord's neck. The Vortigern sucked in a deep and urgent breath as his face left the puddle. He had been moments from death, and panic was strong on him.

'Strip these men and place them in that building yonder. Post four guards outside their holding cell. Check them periodically. Do not let them speak. If they do not obey, cut out their tongues.'

The warriors nodded their understanding, and removed the Britons from the courtyard. Aelle looked at the wretched lord lying in the mud, then grinned at him.

The Vortigern winced as he was dragged to his feet. All the fight had left him. He had been so sure of himself just hours past, and now he had lost his fort, his kingship and his soldiers - his dignity seemed a distant memory.

How fast fortunes can change, thought Aelle, as he dragged the man to the wall, tied a noose around his neck and threw the tail end up to a warrior on the parapet. The Saxon caught it, quickly took in the slack, pulled the Vortigern on to his tiptoes and then tied off the rope solidly.

'You will now give me all of the information I will need to take these lands,' whispered Aelle menacingly. 'Anything I ask, you will tell me. If you do not, I will slowly flay you alive. If you answer me well, I will reward you with a quick death. The choice is yours.'

The Vortigern put up no resistance, and answered Aelle's questions thoroughly: Who were the overlords at the other fortifications in the area? Which was the strongest? Which was the weakest? What were the layouts and weaknesses of the other forts? How did they communicate with each other? Were any soldiers expected to report in this day? The questions went on for hours, and the Vortigern answered them all. Finally, when Aelle could think of no more, he slit the man's throat with no preamble, held his head back as the blood flowed, and thanked him.

He put his lips next to the man's ear as he spoke. 'With the information you have given me, I will take your lands and your people will be butchered to make room for my own. My thanks to you, Vortigern.'

A final look of horror formed in the dying man's eyes as the light dimmed within them and blood poured freely down his chest. Aelle released his grip, and the Vortigern's head slumped forward. With his spirit full of terror, his life left his body.

Epilogue...

In the following years, many more Saxons flooded into the valley, and Aelle conquered another of the Britons' hill forts. The citizens began to flee to the west, seeking sanctuary with their fellow Britons, who long ago had occupied the mighty stone castles the Romans had built in the lands of Cornwallium. They knew that these fierce barbarians would defeat them if they remained and attempted to fight them, and as more of the Saxon warbands flooded into the area, their chances of victory dwindled evermore.

One fort, however, seemed utterly impossible to defeat. It was so well defended that even a small band of trained warriors could hold the ground against the Saxons for many years to come. A large group of Romano-Britons had wisely banded together there. Aelle discovered that the overlord at that fort was a man called Finn, and that he would be no easy target. Finn was from true Roman fighting stock. He and his warriors were disciplined and well dug in. It would take more than brute force to take his high fort and seize the port of Ipwinesfleet. Aelle plotted and planned, then sent messages home to his kinsmen, and in the months that followed, Hengist and Horsa arrived on the shores of Sussex.

The treasures beneath the mound remained lost for centuries more, but a great man would soon find Jeshua's covered tomb beside that hidden vault. He would discover the cup and the spear, and that man would revive the waning faith of Christianity in the land. The first Holy Knight had arrived in Sussex...

Galahad
Year 503

Chapter - 6

Galahad
Year 503

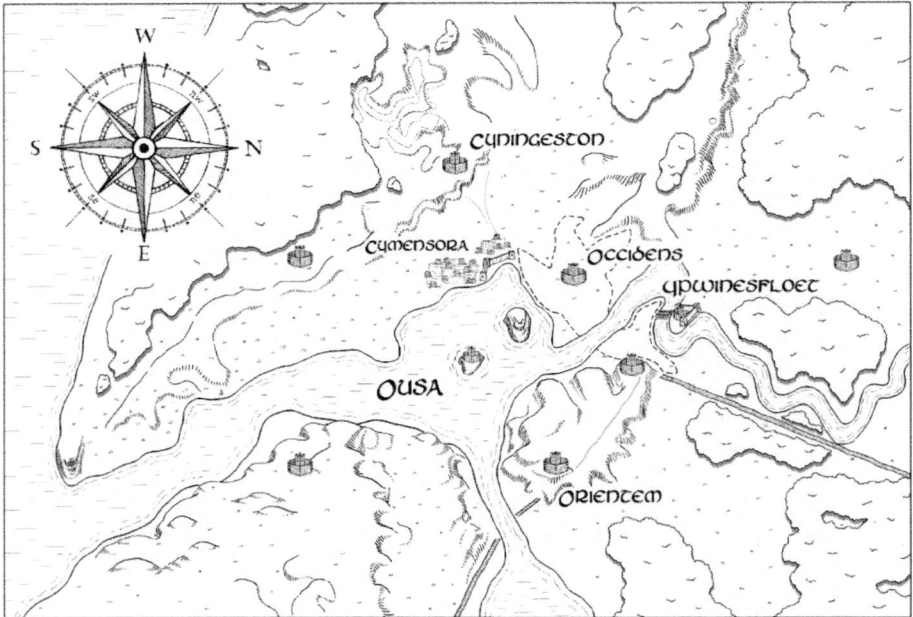

The wind and rain lashed mercilessly at Galahad as he continued to ride towards the east. Random gusts on the exposed hilltops were threatening to unseat him and he was beginning to feel harassed by the weather. Raindrops whipped into the visor of his helmet, stinging his eyes as his horse plodded slowly on. He was not even sure he was heading in the right direction any more, but he understood now that wherever he arrived was most likely the place where he was meant to be. Over the last three years he had been beginning to get a vivid sense that nothing in this world happened purely by chance and he was learning fast to trust his instincts. That did not, however, make his current exposure to the weather any easier to bear. He had been riding for weeks now, questing for the Grail he had envisioned, and he began to wonder how his brothers-in-arms fared in their own quests.

Galahad had left Bors and Percival behind some days ago now. He was sorely missing their company. They were good travel companions, and with them at his side, he had felt less exposed to the dangers of the world. Together, they were a mighty force that few had the nerve to attack head-on, but the dream was clear; he must face this part of his journey alone. Nobody could help him where he was going. His solo journey had led him past the imposing fort at Lyminster, where Uther had slain a very large, fierce dragon during a mighty storm raging there many years past. He had hung it from the town walls and the locals had chanted for him, 'Uther Pend Dragon!' Uther's popularity had grown from that day forward, and soon after, his great reign at Camelot had begun.

Galahad's horse plodded on for what seemed like hours, until at last he caught sight of an orange glow in the distance, tucked away in the woodland up ahead. It looked to be a crofter's hut, he thought, but he could not be sure from this range. Galahad turned his horse, and urged it forward.

As he approached what he now saw was indeed a small rustic dwelling, he caught the scent of smoke coming from a fire within. It conjured ideas of winter, warmth and respite in his tired mind. Galahad could not remember the last time he had slept with a roof over his head; it seemed like an age ago, and he was in sore need of it. He looked to the skies, placed his hands together over his heart, closed his eyes and spoke.

'Father, may this dwelling offer me safety, shelter, warmth and kind folk to aid me on my journey.'

He leaned forward, swung a leg back and slid from the saddle, taking the reins and choosing to walk his steed over the final hillock to the homestead. He did not want to alarm the residents there any more than he was already going to by arriving fully armed and mounted, so he trudged on, the weight of his armour becoming unbearable in his weariness.

The crofter had heard him approaching, and from the doorway, he called out into the night. 'Halt and state your purpose!' he yelled, in a deep, lilting tone.

'Do not fear me, sir, for I mean you no harm,' Galahad replied. 'I have travelled far, and am in sore need of warmth and rest. I have coin and gratitude if you can aid me?'

The crofter remained silent a while, considering the request, then nodded his head, and with an open arm, he gestured for Galahad to enter before disappearing inside. Galahad tied his horse to a fence railing beside the house, offered the beast a sincere apology for his poor lodgings, and promised him much luxury as soon as he was able to provide it. He removed his leather-lined helmet, and his face became cold and wet as the stinging rain hit him full force. Galahad ducked his head under the doorway to escape the onslaught, and stepped inside the small dwelling.

The hut was a simple lodging, but once inside, he could see it had been constructed beautifully. Blissful silence took hold as he shut the door, and the relief at being in a warm and quiet space once again was wonderful. It was sparsely furnished, but each piece of furniture looked to be handmade, and carved with the most exquisitely detailed imagery.

The crofter sat quietly at his table, whittling away intently at a piece of wood. Galahad could not quite see what it was he was making.

'Thank you, kind sir,' he said as he took in his new surroundings, his eyes adjusting to the bright light of the fire after many hours travelling in the dark on a moonless night. 'It is a great relief to be out of the wind and rain. The weather is not kind this night and your hospitality is greatly appreciated. I hope I am not an imposition to you or your family?'

The crofter continued his carving as he answered, 'No family up here, sir, just me, and should you prove to be an honourable man, then you are also no imposition. May I help you with your armour Sir Knight?' he asked, turning from his carving to look at him properly for the first time.

Galahad nodded in the affirmative. The burly hermit got up from his seat and began quickly unbuckling the armour straps; removing each piece in the correct order, then laying them neatly on a bench by a wall near the fire.

'My name is Sir Galahad, and I would dearly like to know the name of the man who aids me in my time of need.' He met the man's eyes, and revelled for a moment in the sensation of being free of his armour for the first time in weeks.

'Ah, I am no one these days, Sir Galahad,' the crofter replied, 'but my old family once called me Healfdan.'

He had a strange accent that Galahad had not encountered before. His tone of voice rose and fell in a rhythmic lilt as he spoke.

'A Dane?' Galahad enquired.

'Aye, I am half Dane; my father was from Daneland, but my mother lived on these shores. I have spent much time in both lands, but I have now lived here for much longer than I ever lived in the land of the Danes, so am I now a Briton, Sir Galahad?'

'Perhaps you are,' he replied.

'Perhaps,' Healfdan agreed, 'but truly, I am just another man in this world. I am glad to have abandoned titles in recent years – the world is a confusing enough place, is it not?'

'That it is, sir, that it most certainly is.' Galahad nodded his agreement.

They smiled with good heart at one another, and a bond of trust began to form.

⬦⬦⬦

Once Galahad's armour had been fully removed, Healfdan gestured for him to sit by the fire in a beautifully carved wooden chair he had placed there for him. He did so, and the warmth that began to seep into his bones was so exquisite that Galahad shuddered as it travelled up his body.

'Nothing like a little cold and hardship to make a fire your best friend, eh?' Healfdan remarked.

Galahad nodded again, and looked fondly at this stranger who had welcomed him fearlessly into his home in the middle of the night. He seemed a cheerful fellow, and Galahad began to feel warmly towards him.

'You are an intriguing man, Healfdan. I should like to know more of you if you would be willing?'

Healfdan pulled another chair over to the fire, and sat. He leaned forward and met Sir Galahad's eyes once again, examining him deeply for a few seconds, and then he smiled. 'If you are able to remain awake, you must first tell me your tale, Sir Knight, and then I will tell you mine. What brings you by my home at such a strange hour, and where do you hail from? I will serve us food, and we can talk, should you wish?'

Galahad smiled his thanks and nodded his agreement. While Healfdan ladled some simple stew into two wooden bowls, Galahad began to tell his story.

'I hail from the Cornish lands, and grew up by the sea in a mighty castle on the northern coast. My liege lord is a great man named Artur whose father, King Uther, banded our court of knights together in troubled days gone by. I should like to tell you of Uther's story, Healfdan, but I fear that tale may take many hours to recount to you, so we must save that for another time.' He took a spoonful of stew and found it was delicious. 'For the sake of my own tale, you must only know that he is a mighty king who is much revered; a fair man who attempts to bring some forgotten virtue to the people of the land. Too long were they abandoned to their own fate when the Romans departed our shores. The land was left in sore need of a king to champion its people once again, and that man was King Uther. Under the instruction of a wise druid named Ambrosius Merlinus, he gathered twelve of the greatest knights in the country to his table, and I am the son of one of the first. My father was called Sir Lancelot.'

'I may have heard of him,' interjected Healfdan, raising an eyebrow.

'Aye, I am sure you have, sir, and it is that tale of betrayal you are now recounting to yourself that brought me into this world. I am indeed the product of that illicit affair, and it has haunted me since my birth. I am a bastard, and it has caused me much heartbreak but, Healfdan, I have come to believe that it is precisely that sort of torment that opened the door to my soul. Whoever would have guessed that the entrance to Heaven might be found in Hell?' He shook his head whimsically.

Healfdan reflected on the thought as the fire crackled, and he nodded his head in agreement. Galahad could see in his eyes that Healfdan too had suffered a hard life, and grown wise and strong as a result of it.

'Ambrosius protected me in my early years as he did for Artur, and he helped my mother Elaine with my education as I grew. Now, Healfdan, Ambrosius is a brilliant but frustrating man, always answering questions with riddles, and never offering straight answers. Fine riddles they were, however, and as I attempted to solve each one, unbeknownst to me, a new space in my mind was growing, and it was precisely because of those irritating conundrums that I became able to concentrate much harder and for ever increasing periods of time. Then, after some years of practising this skill, something strange occurred to me. For any question I now had, the answers I needed would just come to me. The trick, it seemed, was simply in recognising them when they came; it's all a matter of timing and attention, you see. He taught me other mysteries too, instructing me with methods to remember my dreams, and then aiding me in their translation as I recounted them to him, and it was a rare vivid dream that brought me here this night.'

Galahad paused and stared at the ceiling as his mind sought out the words he was grasping for. 'Many months ago, I awoke from a deep sleep with visions ringing in my head as I came to. All covered in sweat was I, and my heart and mind took many moments to recognise my surroundings as my awareness came back into this world. I had dreamt of an enormous Eagle with a sweeping tail – enormous, Healfdan! – so big that it seemed a small world was contained within it, and yet, I sensed that this glorious Eagle could not move. I noticed then that it had a broken foot, and in its claws was clutched a glorious golden cup with a red cross at its centre. The cup began to radiate a bright light, pulsing the beautiful colours of a rainbow, faster and faster as it grew in my vision. The light became so bright, it began to hurt my eyes, but I was unable to look away from it. It grew and grew, until I could no longer see anything at all, and for a moment, I was lost. I then found myself arrived by a clear pool of shallow water, and a great bell sounded that rang so loud that it shook the light of the world around me once again. A man appeared to me then, dressed in a rainbow of colour, walking toward me through the pool. I did not recognise him, though I felt he was a good man. He was beautiful, Healfdan, glowing with an energy that I cannot describe with words. He soon stood before me and, slowly, he reached out a hand and tapped his finger between my eyes. Then he vanished. I awoke back in this world, moments later, with tears flowing from me like a river!'

A tear formed now in Galahad's eye as he remembered his dream, and he fell silent for a while as Healfdan waited patiently for him to continue. The fire crackled and popped as the rain lashed down in waves on the roof outside.

'This was unlike any dream I had ever had, Healfdan, the memory of it would not leave my mind as other dreams do. I knew not what to make of it, so I sought out Ambrosius in the cave beneath the castle, knowing well that his sight and understanding was far better than mine in these matters. Once I had recounted my tale, Ambrosius fell silent until I thought he had forgotten I was there with him, but in time, his attention came back to me. He stood and instructed me to follow him, and in short order we found ourselves back inside the castle walls. Ambrosius began shouting at the squires to wake the Knights of Camelot and to bring them, with all haste, to the Round Table for instruction. Once they were gathered together, and with Artur bidding his twelve knights to sit, Ambrosius began to speak.

'"We find ourselves at a critical turning point in history, young knights. A great quest must now be laid before you that will ring out through the ages. Your deeds and bravery must shine forth as I now put you to task. Sir Galahad has had a true vision, and you must all heed my words. You will go forth this very day and search the land for the Grail. It is a fine yet simple vessel, and you will only know the truth of its authenticity once you have found it. It will be a symbol of hope to our people in times to come, and your very seeking of it will change the world in ways you cannot imagine. I know not what perils you may face on your travels, but act like the knights you are on your adventures. Have courage, have honour, watch your words and mind your actions. You must set the highest standards you can dream of as you journey, and when asked for aid, you would do well to obey. Seek your adventures, Sir Knights, and let us see which one of you will find the Grail. If you conquer a knight when challenged, send him to Artur's court as your prize, and we will absorb him into our cause. Should you succeed in your quest, send word, and I will come to you with all haste, but remember, Sir Knights, it is the journey that is most important, and not the destination. Go now, pay attention to what occurs, and see where your hearts will lead you."

'With those words, he bid me join him once again as the knights and squires began to exit the hall. Once they had departed, he spoke to me in confidence. "Galahad, an arduous journey lies ahead of you, and I have three pieces of advice for you: firstly, you would do well to travel at night; secondly, you would do well to think less and to observe more; and thirdly, you would do well to pay respect to your ancestors!"

'And with those cryptic words ringing in my ears, Ambrosius stood and made his way to the door, then turned and left me with this parting riddle. "The eagle in the west will be found to the east, and the crippled man will lead you where others cannot travel."

'So, heeding his words, I made myself ready, and as the sun dipped below the horizon, I began to journey east with my companions, Sir Bors and Sir Percival. Good men they are and I sorely miss their company. Life is better shared with good companions, is it not, Healfdan?'

Healfdan considered the thought for a moment. 'Sometimes,' he agreed, 'but we must also spend much time alone to discover who we truly are. I find myself enjoying people and crowds less and less these days, but once in a while, I do meet somebody interesting, and it does indeed break up the monotony.'

He smiled kindly, and Galahad continued with his story.

'Around one week ago, after a long night's march, I fell asleep beneath a great oak tree atop a mighty hill as the sun began to show its light in the east. I would rather not discuss the dream I had that morning with you, Healfdan, but it left me with no uncertainty in its translation. I knew then that I should leave my companions to their own adventures, lest my journey may lead them to their doom. It was difficult to go our separate ways, as they are good friends, but once we had parted ways, I began to notice a quieter space forming in my mind, and I then remembered Amrosius' second piece of advice – that I would do well to think less and to observe more. I had never chosen to spend much time on my own, and I must admit that quiet observation was much easier to practice without daily conversations, and the processing of others' thoughts. Alas, I have spent so many days in silence recently, I fear I now talk too much. Apologies for my prattling, Healfdan.'

Healfdan clapped his hands together in appreciation of Galahad's story, and leaned back in his chair, smiling. 'Fear not, my friend; your story is well received.' He stretched his legs out and clasped his hands together in his lap. 'I too have been many weeks without conversation, and I do appreciate a good story and a break from my own company. Unlike most people, Galahad, I have always enjoyed extended periods of silence.' He shrugged his confusion. 'I grew up in very remote lands where people and conversation were not often available, you see, but now the world is becoming a busy place, is it not?'

Galahad nodded his agreement.

'With the big settlements cropping up all over the country, I was beginning to find it difficult to escape from people for long, but few folks are willing to travel the windswept high hills these days, which is why I chose to build my home here. I tire of dealing with people and their ever predictable ways. For the most part, they are a greedy self-interested lot, are they not, Galahad? Continually looking for what can be gained from their interaction with you. Slowly attempting to drain some benefit or service from you that they would rather steal from your presence than work towards themselves. Foolish folk, they are, but I hope they will learn one day that the world will always reflect their lacking straight back to them. Equally, though, I have seen that even a beast can find a way to be a saint if they can but change their viewpoint. 'Tis a strange paradox, this world.' He shook his head and sighed. 'It is not often I meet a being made whole, Galahad, so I thank you for your company, and now you have told me your tale I feel we were fated to meet this night. You travel on to Mutuantonis, do you not?'

Galahad was not quite sure he understood anything Healfdan was saying, but he nodded his head with some surprise as he registered the accurate foretelling of his destination. It was one of the few places that Galahad knew of in this part of the country, and he had indeed decided to head that way.

'I have spent much time there, Galahad, and it is a place filled with an energy unlike any other I have encountered. Much has occurred there, and much is yet to occur there, but whilst filled with hidden opportunity, it can be a draining place if you do not keep your wits about you. The spirits of the dead hold sway there, and you would do well to make them your allies.' He leaned forward and adjusted a log in the fire.

'How is it you know whence I travel, Healfdan?' enquired Galahad, bewildered.

'Your dream, Sir Galahad, and the words of your mage Ambrosius. "I believe what you seek will be found in the west." The Romans once called the fort atop the great hill mound by the port "Occidens", which means "west" in Latin, as it is sited on the western side of the escarpment. The fort on the eastern side is called "Orientem", which translates to "east". I believe that as the town started to grow on the shore opposite Occidens, it also took on the name. I believe the Gauls now refer to the old town of Mutuantonis as 'L'ouest'. I also know of the Eagle there, but I will let you discover that for yourself, young Knight. And then there is the Fisher King. Have you heard of Finn the Fisher King, who holds sway in those lands, Galahad?

Galahad shook his head.

'He lives in a wooden fort on a small promontory, which juts out into an estuary there spanned by a mighty stone bridge. It guards the entrance to a major port in the area called Ipwinesfleet. Finn was cruelly injured by a knife wound to the lower back in a brutal act of betrayal by the Swedes, Hengist and Horsa. They came to him and sued for peace, so Finn agreed to receive them. Once inside his walls and with treachery in their hearts, they drew their long knives and butchered the court. The Fisher King alone escaped with his life and found sanctuary at his brother Eliazar's fortress. Filled with rage, he gathered a mighty force of knights and retook the land stolen from him there in an act of violent warfare the Saxons had not thought the Britons capable of. Once he had won back his fortress, he persecuted the Saxons for their betrayal, and cut off all supply lines and trade routes to them. Only the Britons can trade and own land there now.

The Saxons have become prisoners in their own forts, and now call him "Pelles", which means "rock" in their tongue, as he will not be moved on this matter. Finn's wound did not heal well, and in time he became unable to walk. Now he sits silently at the foot of the Eagle, surrounded by guards, unable to enjoy life, in constant pain, and looking out to those enemy forts with distrust in his heart. He sits on the bridge, day after day, pretending to fish there. It is a known pretence; he simply will not allow the Saxons to enter his realm, so he watches all who cross into his lands, waiting for the next attack to come, and no longer willing to work towards peace with any foreigners who approach his home. Betrayal has consumed him. He is now a bitter man.'

Deep in his heart, Galahad knew that Healfdan was sage, and that he must seek out this Fisher King, but it did not sound like he was going to receive a very warm reception.

Healfdan stood. 'You must sleep, Sir Galahad. The sun will soon be rising, and you must be sore tired, so please, lie on my bed and make yourself comfortable. I have much to do once the light arrives. Living alone up here requires much labour, but the benefits outweigh the drawbacks.'

Galahad nodded his agreement and offered his heartfelt thanks. It was only a moment after his head touched the pillow that he was fast asleep. Healfdan unfolded a clean blanket and laid it gently over the sleeping knight. Gathering his axe and his flask, and shoving an apple into his mouth, he headed off deep into the great woods to continue work on his hunting hide, even further afield from established trails and the confusion of humanity. He didn't really need it, but it was always good to be busy, and he enjoyed the work.

Galahad awoke to blissful darkness and silence just after midday. It was strange how quickly he had become used to spending his waking hours in the late evening, and beginning his day when most folk were halfway through theirs. He had been spending so much time in silence and darkness recently that he was beginning to notice qualities within it. Some places had very different qualities of silence than others, and this place was truly peaceful. Despite it being midday, the walls were thick and the roof so well thatched that not a breath of sound or sunlight made its way inside. It was somewhat like a cave in here, he thought, as he stumbled over to where he thought the shutters to the lone window would be found. He located the catch and bright light flooded into the room as he opened it. Galahad winced momentarily at the brightness that assailed him, but then closed his eyes and revelled in the warmth of the sun. It was no mean feat to construct a building so well insulated from the outer world, and he was truly grateful for it. He felt refreshed and at ease. Healfdan had been a far better host than Galahad could have ever hoped for.

'Thank you, Father,' he said, his hands clasped together over his heart.

Leaving his armour stacked neatly on the bench nearby, he opened the door and stepped outside. It was a sunny, warm day, with a cool breeze coming in from the coast. Galahad took a great breath into his nostrils, smelled the scent of the woodland that surrounded him, and smiled. The view from the front door was beautiful. He looked down the chalky, thin trail that ran up the steep slope leading to the hut, and saw that Healfdan had cleared a great deal of the woodland on that slope. Beyond the path, the land stretched on into rolling hills and beautiful forest as far as his eyes could see.

A sparrow darted across his vision, coming so close to him that he could feel the wind of its wings on his face. He smiled heartily, and let out an exclamation of good cheer. 'Ho, little sparrow!' he exclaimed merrily, although the bird was now long gone.

Galahad went and looked to his stallion, greeting him fondly and rubbing his long, noble nose with great affection. He reached into the saddlebag and pulled a few handfuls of oats out for the animal, then extended his tether so he could graze at the long grass. From the corner of his eye, Galahad saw a small garden to the side of the building. He found he could not contain his curiosity, and went off to see what Healfdan was growing there. He had done a spectacular job, he thought, as the plot came into view. There were vegetables of all sorts in raised beds, surrounded by wicker hurdles to contain the earth within. There were neat units of turnips and onions, radishes and burdock, parsnips, cabbages and beets. They looked well cared for and plentiful. Galahad had witnessed how much work was required to grow good vegetables, and his estimation of Healfdan grew ever higher. It was then that he thought he heard the sound of trickling water, and went off to investigate.

Just behind the garden, he saw a tiny stream was running from a tapped spring. The clear water fell into a small stone pool, then flowed off down the hill. Surrounding it, Galahad saw that herbs and flowers had been planted, their reflections beautifully mirroring on the rippling surface. On a flat stone next to the pool, he noticed a wooden bucket and a ladle with a carved long handle. The ladle had been fashioned to look like a small snake had coiled itself around it, with the head dipping into the rim of the bowl. Galahad picked it up gently and dipped it carefully into the water, then raised it to his lips and drank. The water was cold and deeply refreshing, quickly working its way through his tired limbs. He drank again, then filled the bucket, stood off a little distance, removed his clothes and began to ladle the water over his head, scrubbing himself with his hands as he sluiced away the sweat of many days in the saddle. New life flowed through him after the wash.

The sun was high and hot where it could penetrate through the trees, so Galahad filled the bucket again, provided his horse with a good drink, then filled it once more and washed his clothes, wringing them out then hanging them up to dry. He sat naked in the sunlight for a short while, thoroughly enjoying the peaceful place he had found himself in and ever grateful for it.

His trews and undershirt were wearable in no time at all, the breeze and bright sunshine quickly drying his clothes as he sat in silence beneath the shade of the woodland canopy. Getting dressed once again, he began to wonder when Healfdan would return, and how he could thank him. He looked around, and noticed an axe and a pile of logs to the rear of the shelter, so he set to work splitting and stacking the firewood as thanks for his warm welcome. It was good to use his muscles properly after sitting aimlessly in a saddle for so long, and he quickly worked his way through the pile of sawn rounds.

When he was finished, he washed his upper body of sweat once more, and with no sign of Healfdan appearing any time soon, Galahad took his armour out into the sunshine to inspect and polish it while he waited. Before long he had finished that job too. He was grooming his horse; brushing out the dirt that had flicked up on to him as they had ridden and giving his coat a smooth, black, glassy sheen when Healfdan returned.

'Ho, Galahad, how fares you?' enquired Healfdan, waving as he arrived home.

Galahad felt like he was being greeted by an old friend, and offered Healfdan a goodhearted smile and a wave in return.

'I fare well, Healfdan, thanks to you. I feel most fortunate to have found my way to you and your hospitality. I hope you do not mind, but I was very thirsty, and helped myself to water from your spring. I must also confess, I had a look around your garden while I attended to my upkeep. You have a beautiful home here.'

Healfdan waved away Galahad's concern. 'Do not worry yourself, Sir Galahad, there are few folk I enjoy the company of for very long, but I feel at ease in your presence – you seem to be a good man.'

'As do you, sir,' Galahad replied, bowing flamboyantly in jest.

They chuckled together like old friends.

'It is good to be in the high hills again,' remarked Galahad.

'Aye, it is a magical spot, is it not?'

'That it is, Healfdan, that it most certainly is!' the knight agreed wholeheartedly.

As the sun dipped below the hills to the west, Healfdan shared some fresh, hot stew with Galahad, then aided him as he attempted to fix his armour back on. Galahad's mind was clear, his body well rested and fed, his armour shone and his stallion was groomed and saddled. He felt like a new man. Seeking out his coin purse from his saddlebag, he proffered three gold coins to Healfdan; a small fortune!

'Please accept these coins, Healfdan. I carry much wealth and have little need of it. Never have I been so grateful for a warm welcome or a place to lay my head, so please take this from me. I would like to see you well.'

Healfdan reached forward and closed Galahad's fingers back over the coins. 'My thanks to you for your kind offer, Galahad, but my aid to you requires no payment. Your company and your tale I will treasure always, but my aid to one such as you will ever come at no cost! A true friendship cannot be bought, Sir Knight, and I would rather have a friend of you than make our meeting a dealing. Promise me you will stop and say hello if you ever find yourself in these parts again, and we will call it even!'

Galahad embraced Healfdan with genuine appreciation. 'You are a fine man, Healfdan, and I would be honoured to call you my friend. Would but the world had more like you in it! I will indeed come back this way should I succeed in my quest, and I will seek you out to tell you what occurred on my return. Let us see what fate decrees!'

'That would be most agreeable, Sir Knight,' replied Healfdan, though sadly, he knew that he would never see him again.

They smiled warmly at each other. Galahad mounted his steed, and with a reluctance to depart that beautiful place deep within his bones, his heels knocked the animal into a walk and he continued his journey east.

Later that evening, Healfdan saw the great pile of split logs stacked neatly to the rear of his dwelling, and atop that pile of logs were three gold coins. He smiled widely and let out a roaring laugh. Healfdan picked up the coins, then went to his treasury beneath a great tree some minutes' walk from his dwelling. He dug out the large chest hidden there. Brushing away the mud, he unlocked the trunk and opened the lid to reveal the small fortune contained within. In that sturdy chest was the crown and wealth of a king! He dropped the three coins in, closed the lid and reburied it all, expertly disguising the disturbed earth with fallen leaves and brush. He said a quick prayer for his father and mother, then headed back to his dwelling to prepare his next meal; for as beautiful as it was, money was not much use to him up there. He could not eat gold.

Galahad rode for many nights, until at last, cresting an enormous downland hill, and as the light of dawn rose slowly in the east, he saw it: the enormous tidal sea estuary of the Ouosa in the far distance. Along the hilltops on either side of the channel he saw mighty wooden fortresses that had the distinctive Roman architecture his ancestors were so famous for. Galahad knew that those forts had once housed vast numbers of Roman soldiers, but some had been conquered by the Saxons. People now suspected the Roman legions would never return; news of their grim fate had trickled over from distant shores in the years following their departure.

The remaining Romano-Britons left behind in this land had gathered together quickly and from far afield to make use of those fortifications once the army had abandoned them to their fate. Most had fled to Cornwallium to unite behind mighty stone walls, but some had remained and fought for their ancestral homes. There were few places left in this part of the country that were as defensible as this mighty sea channel with its steeply rising hills, but the stubborn and foolish folk who had not banded together in the forts here, and many of the weaker burghs surrounding the hills, had been quickly overrun by Saxon and Danish invaders once their weakness had been exposed. Now, after many hard years of struggle, the Saxons and Britons were living side by side in an uneasy alliance, but the land continually hovered on the brink of war.

Torchlight on the ramparts could still be made out in the early morning light, and Galahad thought he saw the slow movement of watchmen on the walls. The forts were on high bluffs on either side of the estuary, and seemed to stretch far inland. The lookout towers were primed; ready to light warning beacons from their prominent locations should any enemy ships be seen coming into their territory. Warships and troops could then be assembled rapidly from the great ports of Ipwinesfleet and Cymensora at the end of the channel. Due to this ability to warn against impending attack, their might in gathered numbers, highly defensible forts and quick response time, they had held fast against all further attacks from the marauding Swedes, Danes and Gauls so keen on the quick plunder they had succeeded in acquiring all along the British coastline. Galahad turned his horse to the left to follow the hill-ridge inland, through the settlement of Occidens and on to the seaport at Ipwinesfleet.

A half-day's ride over sweeping hills with the estuary at his right brought him further along the downlands to one of the greatest of the many forts set along the hilltops in that land. The Saxons that occupied it now called it Kingston or 'Cyningeston' in the old tongue. It had one of the steepest hills in the region at its eastern side, dropping down to a large stretch of land where the town itself was located, bordering the estuary and one of the larger seaports on the channel. Galahad had learned that this port was called Cymensora. Ipwinesfleet, or Ypwinesfloet as the Saxons called it, was to be found further inland. The great fort on top of the bluff here had been turned into what looked like a wooden castle, with parapets and a large stockade surrounding a vast area of the hilltop. The locals had named it Castle Hill. There were large, ancient burial mounds on and surrounding that high rise. Galahad did not know how old they were, but for one reason or another, none had dared to rob those mounds; even the plundering Romans had left them alone. Because of this seemingly sacred and protected ground, the local warlords were now adding their own burial mounds amongst the old as each regional king passed away, safe in earth that none had yet dared to dig in. Healfdan was right, thought Galahad – the dead held sway here, and woe would befall any folk who would desecrate those graves!

He skirted the stockade some distance from it, garnering much attention from the Saxon watchers on the walls, who were clearly curious about this shiny knight passing by on his jet-black steed. Galahad did not want to stop and talk; he had a destination in mind and plenty of time left to get there that day, so he urged his horse down the frighteningly steep slope and cantered on towards Occidens.

It was not long before he came to the next fortification, located at the head of the town. There was a large settlement there not far from the coastline at Cymensora. The Romans had also constructed a large burial and cremation ground here for the local townspeople, which was still in use. There was another large stockade surrounding the town fortification here; but the buildings were now bleeding outside those defensive structures, down the slope towards the narrower sea inlet that led to the port of Ipwinesfleet. The Romans had also cobbled together a small wooden fortress in the town centre, which sat atop an enormous mound of earth. There seemed to be no stone quarries in the immediate area, so this was obviously the best they could manage. He could not be sure if the fort was constructed on a manmade or a natural mound, but it provided incredible views across all of the surrounding town, and far across the downs.

As he cantered on down the main thoroughfare of Occidens, Galahad noticed more burial mounds and another mighty fort in the distance to the east; it was set atop another enormous chalk bluff that looked down on to Ipwinesfleet. He marvelled for a moment at this incredible valley filled with ancient burials and mighty fortresses. The living and the dead were crammed in side by side here, and Galahad sensed this land had been occupied for a very long time. He could not deny that it was quite clearly a very attractive location to settle in, with its green and wooded, almost mountainous hills rolling in from the ocean.

With great relief, he saw at last that in the valley to the north-east his destination was in sight. It looked to be an extensive harbour at the end of the vast tidal inlet, with freshwater tributaries feeding into it from the north, surrounded either side by vineyards and farmland. The Romans had been known to grow vast quantities of grapevines here, he had been told; it was thought that wine of the greatest quality had been made at Ipwinesfleet for many centuries, and no matter how many battles had ensued there, few it seemed were willing to destroy that heritage.

He trotted on down the well-established roads, and puzzled at the strange layout of the town. It was unlike any road system he had seen the Romans construct elsewhere in the country. They were very fond of their straight roads, he knew, but apart from the main thoroughfare that snaked its way through the centre of the town in a roughly straight line, that did not seem to be the case here. Perhaps the tracks and borders that marked out the town had been there long before the Romans had arrived, he theorised.

Galahad could now make out the mighty stone wall, and the incredibly large bridge that spanned a vast curve in the channel at the end of the estuary, crossing from one shore to the other to connect the two valleys either side of the sea. The construction was magnificent, providing a truly safe harbour behind that enormous and nigh-impossible feat of blockwork. The Romans were extraordinary builders, he thought again, but they had taken that knowledge with them. Galahad wondered how many years it might take to reach those heights of engineering in the country once more.

As he neared the coastline, he acknowledged a stroke of luck, realising that he would not need to use the bridge himself, as the promontory of Ipwinesfleet and the fortification upon it were at the end of the sea channel on his side of the river. Many boats were harboured on both sides of the bridge. There were beautiful masted sailing vessels of many varying shapes and sizes moored along the wharfs.

Galahad trotted on inland, and then followed the coastline to his right until he reached the outskirts of the port. This was a busy place indeed; people gaped and gawked at him as he rode through the surrounding settlements on the well-established trails. They had seen knights before, of course, but Galahad was a big man; he set a fine figure in his gleaming silver armour, and he looked quite unlike any of the soldiers in this part of the land. Shortly thereafter, he came to the foot of the large wall and found himself before the sturdy wooden gates set in its centre. He assumed that this was the same wall that led to the bridge. It was a truly fabulous defensive structure.

With no greeting forthcoming, Galahad called up to the watchman on the parapet. 'I seek the Fisher King!' he shouted loudly.

'And who might you be?' bellowed back the guard as his head appeared over the edge of the defences.

'My name is Sir Galahad. I have travelled long and far from the Cornish lands to the west on a mission of grave importance. I must speak with the Fisher King!' he repeated.

The guard disappeared behind the wall for a moment, then reappeared and shouted down to Galahad. 'The Fisher King does not like uninvited guests, Sir Galahad, but I have sent word to him and we shall see what his response will be. Wait there until I receive my instruction.'

He disappeared again. Galahad's stallion skittered sideways impatiently as they waited. He quickly tired of the animal's meanderings, and slid from the saddle to hold the horse by the reins; it seemed like an age before the guard reappeared with a simple statement.

'You may enter!' he bellowed, and the gates eased slowly open to reveal the small jut of land before him and the great sea harbour which surrounded it.

Galahad entered through the archway. From his high vantage point, he saw a simple trading post down by the docks, a small dwelling for the harbourmaster by the wharf and some secure stone storehouses a little further up the slope. There was a moderately sized hall set on the top of the rise, and he assumed that this was the home of the Fisher King.

Galahad halted. He suddenly became aware of a sensation he had not experienced before that day. He knew with certainty that he had never been to this part of the country before, and yet he was now struck with an odd feeling of nostalgia. He could not forge any clarity into that supposition, but the feeling was strong on him as he looked around curiously, pondering on the odd sensation.

He turned to look behind him, and saw that stone steps had been set on the inside of the vast wall, providing access to the walkway that led down to the bridge. The Fisher King had imposed a toll on the use of that bridge, but other than travelling across the bay on a slow punt, it was the only crossing point available. He did not charge fortunes to use it, but the volume of traffic it received was making the Fisher King a very wealthy man. The promontory itself was heavily defended on all fronts, and the bridge and walls created an impenetrable bottleneck into the lands beyond. A great Roman road arrived here from Londinium, and a network of freshwater rivers the locals called the 'Middle Winders', or the 'Midwindes', convened a little further inland. Galahad remembered it had been named thus as this place was considered the centre of Britannia in Roman times. Freshwater and seawater met here, the valley opened up here, the roads all led here. This was truly one of the most important places in the kingdom. Galahad had never seen so many people in one place before, and it made his head spin. There were hundreds of folk on the far shores, working on the docks and the hilltop. The court of Artur occupied one of the greatest castles Galahad had ever laid his eyes upon, but the population there was tiny compared to this.

A guard gestured for Galahad to follow him, and he led his horse along the slope to the small wooden hall. There was very little stone to quarry in those lands, so most of the buildings here were made of ash and oak. The great port wall was constructed of flint and mortar, and the bridge itself appeared to be made of sandstone blocks the early Romans had most likely quarried from further inland. It also looked like a considerable amount of the surrounding forests had been cut down in the valley floors for lumber and firewood. The stripped land had then been turned into farms and mighty vineyards long ago.'

As they neared the hall, Galahad noticed what seemed to be an ancient graveyard nearby, its tombstones were falling apart and covered in blackberry thorns. A beautiful, large yew tree was also growing there that appeared to be very ancient. The two guards outside the hall eyed Galahad warily as they took the reins of his horse, and gestured for him to enter.

It was gloomy inside. A sombre atmosphere struck him as Galahad's eyes fell upon the Fisher King, sitting stock still atop a raised platform ahead of him. A fire burned weakly in the centre of the hall, and the acrid smoke stung his eyes as he squinted into the gloom, hoping to make out some detail in the features of the king. An oppressive air of misery hung about him, and no warmth shone from his stone-dead eyes.

The Fisher King spoke slowly, in deep, lifeless tones. 'Sir Galahad, I have very little patience these days – I entertain your presence only out of respect to your mother, so state your purpose, then begone from my hall.'

'My mother?' Galahad asked, perplexed.

The king remained silent for an uncomfortable amount of time, and then answered with an intense look in his eyes, 'Your mother is my daughter, Galahad – you are my grandson. It surprises me not that she did not talk of me. We parted ways on bitter notes when you were just a babe. Now, what do you want of me?'

Galahad was stunned that his mother had not told him of their connection, and he was greatly saddened at the lack of warmth being offered to him by his grandfather. He had many questions then, but he caught himself, and stated his purpose.

'I seek the Grail, King Finn, and I suspect it is to be found here. Do you have possession of it, sir?'

'I know not of what you speak, Galahad,' he replied shortly.

Galahad waited for more, but nothing came forth, so he continued. 'I believe it is a cup or a vessel of some sort. It is to be of great importance in times to come, and I have been compelled to seek it here. I would ask your permission to do so if you would allow me?'

The Fisher King shuddered slightly, and Galahad assumed it was from the pain of his wound. He seemed lost in himself once again, but after a moment, he replied, 'There is no such item in my possession, Galahad, and I would certainly know of it if it was held in my lands, but I grant you permission to search the grounds here, should you wish?'

A fleeting picture of the graveyard and the yew tree flashed into Galahad's mind, and he blinked rapidly from the strange vision. He had been experiencing a rather peculiar sensation since he had arrived on the promontory, and now he was also mildly confused at the sudden change in demeanour that had come over the Fisher King; he did not seem any warmer, but he was far more agreeable to his presence all of a sudden, and Galahad found that rather odd. However, he did not want to push the issue further when he had been granted a chance to seek the Grail in these lands, so he decided not to press for more answers, and to make the most of the opportunity presented to him.

Galahad bowed to the king. 'My thanks to you, King Finn. I will disturb you no longer, and will inform you if I succeed in my search. If I do not succeed, I will inform you of my departure, should that be agreeable to you?'

The Fisher King nodded his head. 'Good luck, Sir Knight,' he said amiably, and as Galahad departed, he paused once again, feeling like he was certainly talking to a different man than the one he had met on his entrance.

Galahad retrieved his horse and led it over to the yew tree, where he secured the reins. He sat down beneath the tree for a while and examined the graveyard more closely. It was sad to see it in such a state. Christianity had taken a firm hold of the populace in Cornwallium. Many churches had been built in those lands, but they seemed few and far between here. Galahad then considered the possibility that perhaps there may have been a church set next to this graveyard once upon a time, so he got up to go and look around.

After a brief inspection, he noticed that there was a small area of land that seemed to have no gravestones present in it at all, but was surrounded by them. The thorn bushes and grass also seemed stunted in that area. It was reasonably close to the edge of the promontory, which dropped down steeply to the estuary below. As he looked closer, he noticed that the land between the possible former structure and the steep promontory wall was also utterly bereft of graves and seemed to have very little vegetation growing in it in comparison to the surrounding ground. He called one of Finn's guards over to him; two of them had been watching Galahad quizzically, clearly confused at what the strange knight was doing.

'What do you know of this graveyard?' he enquired.

The guard looked perplexed, but answered him nonetheless. 'It has been here since I can remember, Sir Knight. We assumed there must have been a tiny church located here in times gone by. There is a big church at the foot of the town now, but it is not well used; since the Saxons began to arrive on our shores, most of the Christian townsfolk fled to the north and the west. There are still a few brave followers of Christ here, but they are a shunned lot who keep mostly to themselves. They struggle to fit in amongst the pagan warriors but are tolerated well enough these days. Much blood has been shed in the name of both of their beliefs, but it seems an uneasy balance has been struck, at least for now, anyhow.'

'And the king?' asked Galahad. 'Which belief does he follow?'

'He does not speak of either, sir. He does not speak of much at all these days. He offers sacrifices to the serpents that infrequently appear in the harbour below, but he has no reverence for them. He has simply found that if he feeds them well they do not disturb the local populace. If he does not feed them, then the beasts hunt any flesh they can find. I feel the locals would rather them dead, but none are brave enough to attempt to kill them; they have an armoured hide, and a poisonous bite that leads to a painful death, by all accounts.'

'Aye,' Galahad replied. 'I have had dealings with the beasts; even a lance struggles to pierce their hide.'

The guards took in the measure of Galahad once more; he had clearly risen in their estimation.

'It is a sad existence, Sir Galahad. Finn sits and broods silently for countless hours. I worry for him; he is in great pain from the wound and the betrayal he suffered at the hands of the Swedes. A great anger is bottled up inside him. He lets no Saxons enter his land or cross his bridge and trade with the Britons inland. The tensions are rising, and it is only a matter of time before they attack his forces here. The Saxon populace are beginning to suffer the consequences of the actions of Hengist and Horsa; they will not tolerate it for much longer, I fear. It would seem that war will soon be upon us once again.' He shook his head, sadly.

A cry of alarm suddenly sounded from inside the hall; they both turned their heads and sprinted back to the building to see what had occurred. Together, they threw open the doors and saw that the king was slumped in his chair with his head resting on his chest; he was not moving. The guard by the door inside the hall cried out to them fearfully as they entered, 'I think the King is dead! I came to check inside, and found him like this. There is a pool of blood at his feet!'

Galahad stepped closer to the king and saw that there was indeed a deep red stain on the platform beneath his chair. He glanced around the room, seeking for any sign of intrusion, but could see nothing untoward. He noticed then the glint of steel in the lap of the king, and went to him. He took the weathered old hand, turned it face up, and pulled back the sleeve to reveal the clean, deep incision on his wrist. He checked the other hand and found the same. There was no sign of struggle, and Finn looked calm. It appeared he had taken his own life.

Galahad was shocked. Not at the sight of death – he had witnessed and taken part in mortal combat more times than he could now remember. No, he was shocked because he suddenly became aware that it was his arrival here that had triggered this turn of events. It felt as if the Fisher King had been waiting for him before he ended his life, and as the thought struck him, Galahad understood clearly. Finn had been presented with an heir, a man of his blood to take over his reign at Ipwinesfleet. He had then decided to release himself from his crippled body. He had made sure his words to Galahad were brief, and that the guards inside the hall would hear them as he spoke. Galahad had been clearly announced as Finn's grandson by the king; therefore he was the rightful heir to his throne. As if in concert with his own thoughts, the guards inside the hall also remembered what had been said, sunk to their knees, and bowed their heads in allegiance. In a most unexpected turn of events, Galahad had quite suddenly become a king.

In the following days, somewhat daunted and confused by his new position in the world, Galahad officially took on his new title. His first task was to bury King Finn, so he ordered his men to begin clearing the graveyard on the promontory and to tidy and preserve the remaining gravesites. Once this was completed, it became quite clear that a small church had indeed once stood in the area he had identified earlier. It was also confirmed that the space directly behind the church that adjoined the steep slope was clear of interments too, so Galahad ordered a grave to be dug there for Finn.

As his men began the task, they noticed that underneath the top layer of soil there seemed to be a thick layer of rubble and loose chalk that was very easy to remove. Curious now, Galahad ordered his men to continue digging, and within the day they had excavated the area to the edges of what seemed to be well-cut, solid walls hewn directly into the earth. By the middle of the second day, they had come across the entrance to what appeared to be an old Roman mortuary tomb, and once enough of the rubble had been cleared away, they called to Galahad who had been watching the excavation keenly. They had broken through into a void beyond.

Galahad lit a torch and passed it to one of his men. Clambering over the remaining scree in the doorway, he entered the tomb, then turned and retrieved the light. He told his men to wait at the entrance and walked slowly inside, looking keenly for any clues to the origins of this space. The torchlight flickered gently in the quiet crypt beneath the earth. Cautiously, he eased his way along the narrow tunnel and saw there was a passage that led to his right. He entered it and arrived inside a large vaulted chamber. There were recesses set into the walls here, and it seemed that many ossuary boxes had been placed within them. And then, at the far end of the tomb, his torchlight flickered on reflected gold. With adrenaline flooding his body, he moved toward it.

As he approached the recess, he saw there was another intricately carved ossuary box set there and a beautiful, yet simple golden chalice with a red cross on its side, was standing proudly on top of it. In stunned silence, and with wide eyes, he realised that this was most certainly the cup he had seen in his vision; there was no doubt about it. The torchlight flickered gently on the unusual vessel as he picked it up and blew off the dust. It was beautiful. Galahad became mesmerised by it for a while; it seemed to exude a certain tingling sensation that he could not put into words. To the right of the recess he saw a long iron spearhead had been placed on a stone shelf, so with his free hand he reached for it. As he did so, he cut his finger on the blade and sucked in a quick breath from the stinging incision. It was razor-sharp and showed no signs of rust, yet it had clearly been there for a considerable amount of time. He set the grail cup back down and held his torch closer to the ossuary box to examine the dusty inscription carved on its side. Wiping away the dirt with his sleeve, slowly he began to discern the lettering. It was inscribed in Latin, and read: 'Jeshua, son of Joseph'. Galahad dropped the torch and was plunged into darkness. He froze in place as a surge like lightning coursed through his body, and his mind instantly recalled the astonishing sequence of events that had led him here. It seemed an unfathomable, inescapable destiny had found him, and he now understood what the true Grail was. It was not the cup, it was the holy spirit Himself that had led him here. The King of Kings was somehow working within him!

Epilogue...

During his lifetime, Galahad reignited Christianity in the lands of Sussex. He built a new church on top of the mound and created an access point to the tomb from above. He filled in the entrance to the mortuary tomb once more, and buried King Finn there as he had intended. Just metres away from where they dug, cunningly hidden by the Romans, lay wealth beyond imagining, but it would take another three hundred years for that fabulous treasure to be rediscovered.

Galahad encouraged the Saxons to convert to Christianity, and many began to show interest in the new faith presented to them. He set the example of a great man and a valiant warrior. He commanded great respect, and the Saxons now wished to be more like him.

As he began to remove the restrictions in trade for the pagan warriors on strict conditions of chivalry, in time, the two faiths began to accept one another. Galahad decreed that if any blood was spilled in his lands, it would be met with swift and brutal justice. Many men were executed in his early reign until the Saxons recognised their warring behaviour would not be tolerated any longer. But this did not stop them all; Danish raiders began to attack the lands with fierce regularity. Great battles were fought, and epic war stories were forged and retold throughout the land.

Galahad never saw Healfdan again, but he thought of him often and attempted to find him on many occasions. Sadly, no matter how hard he tried, or however certain he was of his destination, he could not locate the man's home again.

When Galahad died, an old and happy man, he was interred in the tomb alongside Jeshua at his request. He had united two worlds, and reignited Christianity in the south of the country. He had set new standards for the people, and would forever be remembered as a holy warrior knight, who fiercely protected his homeland and man's right to freedom. The Saxons and Britons he had united under his care took control of his lands in his absence. Many had now converted to Christianity, and they protected his church and the secret space beneath it with fierce pride and honour. Galahad had sown the seeds of greatness in them, and the roots had grown strong in his followers.

War tore through the region in the years following Galahad's death. Sea raids and pitched battles occurred with brutal regularity. His knights fared well against the invaders at first, but in time, the great strength he had left in his people was slowly burned, stolen and broken down by invasion after relentless invasion, until a great famine took hold in the land. A new saviour was now needed for the population, and that saviour was a man called Wilfred.

Wilfred
Year 673

Chapter - 7

Wilfred
Year 673

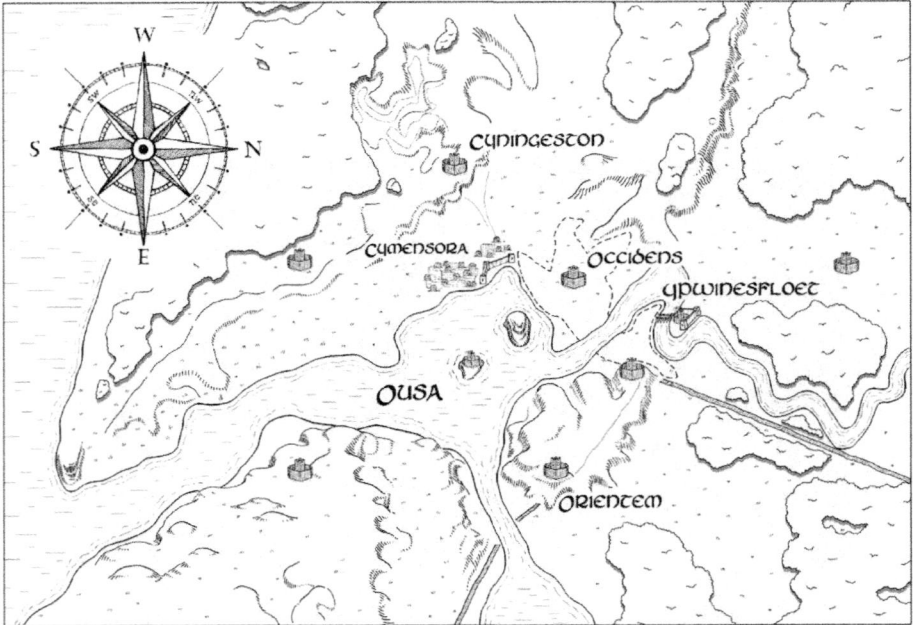

Bishop Wilfred arrived at Ypwinesfloet by road. His feet were blistered and he was deeply tired. He had travelled from York by foot after his banishment from the court of King Egfrid. Wilfred had been too vocal in his thoughts regarding Christianity, and Egfrid had grown tired of the endless debates with his church's lead advisor. The Christians were becoming a law unto themselves and, unable to execute the man for fear of mighty reprisals from the church, Egfrid had banished Wilfred from his presence, never to return.

Wilfred cared little; he was a pious man who saw his banishment and return to poverty as a new opportunity to do something positive in the world. Word had come to him of a great famine occurring in the south of the country, so he had decided to see if he could help the heathen Saxons there. Perhaps if he was able to do so, he could also begin to convert more of the warring folk to Christianity and help to stop the relentless slaughter the Danes brought to those shores, but he had not expected to find the land in such a terrible state. The people were thin! So very thin and, oh, how miserable they looked – like walking corpses. The burial grounds were also filling up fast and, tragically, a great majority of those that had been interred there had taken their own lives to escape the cruel grip of starvation. Those that remained did not look like they were far from making that same choice. Wilfred immediately requested an audience with the King of the South Saxons, and Aethelwalh had agreed.

Grey, heavy clouds covered the sky as Wilfred approached the meeting place at the small church of St Peter atop the promontory. He began to wonder how the people had managed to let themselves fall into such a terrible state. Surely there were many fish in the ocean at their doorstep and plenty of rich land to farm, so why were they starving, he wondered.

Aethelwalh arrived at the church shortly after Wilfred and he was not looking well. He too had not eaten enough to sustain him in what seemed like months now. The misery of his people and the stress of leadership was palpable and hung heavy about him. In desperation, it seemed he had turned back to his old pagan ways, but no amount of sacrifices he had made to the serpents that lived in his lands seemed to be enough to appease the old gods. Raiders were attacking the coast freely, and the people were becoming too weak to hold them off. They were deeply unhappy, and the blame was falling firmly at Aethelwalh's feet.

It had taken more than a century for the Saxons and Britons to unite here, and with the endless infighting and the merciless raids from the Danish during that period the region had weakened considerably. Regular folk – the farmers and tradesmen – had moved away to escape the madness. It was simply no longer safe to work the land, grow crops and raise a family here. As a consequence, the kingdom's grain stores were now dangerously low. Aethelwalh told Wilfred that he had sent traders deeper into Britannia to purchase as much as they could, but the harvest that year had been poor all over the country and little was available for sale.

Wilfred took control of the situation and spoke to Aethelwalh of Christ. He told him that the Lord had sent him to aid them, and that all would be well. He told him that the old gods no longer had the power to save the people in this place, but Jesus both could and would save them, through Wilfred. Aethelwalh must cease sacrificing to the serpents; he must be baptised, then watch and listen to Wilfred as he taught the people of the land how to provide for themselves. The time for war was over, he told him, for always people would return to starvation should the Saxons and Britons not unite. They must work together to produce healthy harvests. If the Saxons put as much effort into farming as they had into war, there would be bountiful food for everyone and the kingdom would flourish once again. Too long had they lived to take and not to create; a terrible famine was the price for that. Aethelwalh listened and agreed. He had little option; nothing he had suggested was working and he feared the people were getting ready to lynch him should their situation not begin to improve.

Epilogue...

Over the following months, Wilfred taught the Saxons how to link their eel nets together to use out at sea. This was a simple way to feed the masses, and only required them working together in two boats to produce fantastic loads of lifesaving fish. He taught them how to farm and tend the land effectively. It was not easy to plough the boggy ground there, so he contrived a way of shoeing and using oxen to do the heavy work as the Saxon gypsy cobs, though beautiful and loyal, were not strong enough to do the job. He showed them how to create enormous, horseshoe eel bends in the river that, once completed, would provide another fast and effortless source of food should they require it. He worked hard for the people there.

During his many years with the South Saxons, Wilfred received word that the exiled King of the Merovingians, Dagobert II, was now attempting to make his way home to eastern France from Ireland. Wilfred greatly admired the works of St Audomer and his connection to the Merovingian line of kings. He was ready to support him in any way that he could. Dagobert II was hoping to raise an army and to reclaim his throne, but he had become mentally unhinged during the last years of his life. He was now a fragile and physically sick man, and his plan was not to be. Dagobert died shortly after arriving at Ypwinesfloet. Wilfred saw him kindly through his final hours, and interred him in the tomb beneath St Peter's. It seemed fitting for another king to join the remarkable men already in that place.

On Wilfred's advice, Aethelwalh began to gather the kings of the region to one common cause, and slowly, with their new united front, they began to butcher the Danish when they came to the southern shores. Outlying settlements became rare, and fortified towns more common. The Danish were now left with no easy targets to exploit, and the raids quickly grew fewer.

The rains came, the crops grew and people converted to Christianity in droves. In a short time, as hunger was replaced by rich harvests, Wilfred became a saint and the kingdoms of Sussex began to thrive. The new concept of united kingdoms began to form in Britain; Aethelwalh and Wilfred had led the way, but it quickly became apparent that giving absolute power to one man was not a good idea. Having many independent rulers kept each regional king in check, but as is the nature of man, it was not long before one man wanted to rule above all others…

Offa
Year 775

Chapter - 8

Offa
Year 775

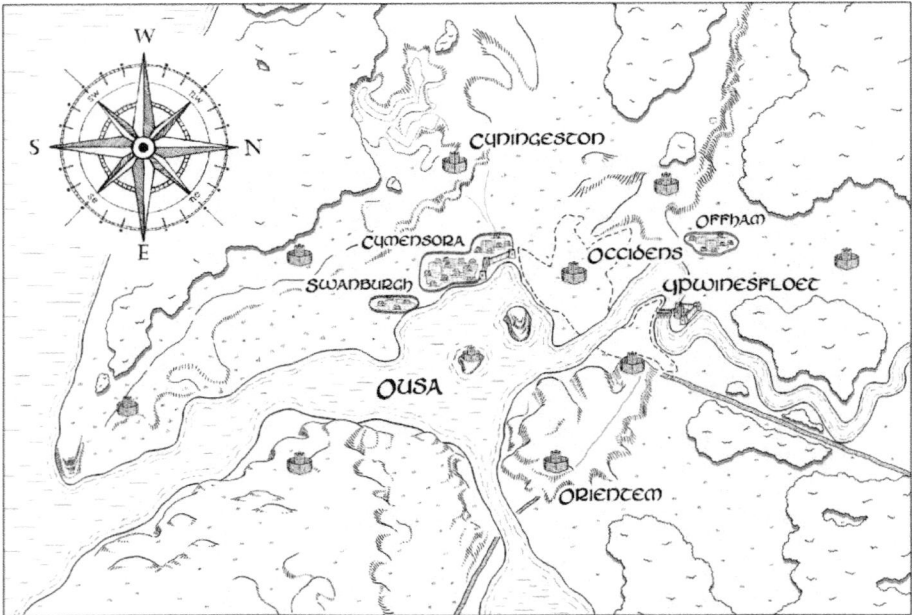

The bright light from the supernova had reached the earth on the previous night, and it was still hanging in the heavens the next evening. Offa pulled his gaze from it once again and spat on the floor. He was devoted to the gods of his ancestors, and he was not happy; the giant red cross that had appeared in the night sky had ignited religious fervour amongst the Christians. They were usually a fearful lot, terrified of their wrathful God and his nailed messenger, but the Christ-followers had become zealots since the cross had appeared in the heavens. Some saw it as a warning, others read it as a blessing, but it had made one undeniable impact on their whole order – it had solidified their certainty that their religion was the right one, and that the truth of their path was now undeniable. All should now follow the way of Christ. To not do so was heresy.

Offa turned his eyes back to the coiled serpent on his newly minted coin and smiled. He had never turned to the Christian God, for he worshipped the serpent gods, and the serpent gods had been kind. He had fought hard and offered many sacrifices to the beasts to create a lasting legacy in his lifetime. He had offered those sacrifices in the name of Odin and Thor and, through his belief in them, they had rewarded him with greatness. He now had two towns named after himself, one in Kent and one in Sussex, both called Offa's Ham, which the locals had now shortened to Offham. He was the greatest ruler Britannia had ever seen, and he had done all of that without a single prayer to the Christian God. He knew his own truth. He believed that there were any number of gods to worship as could be imagined. The mystery was in how to access the powerful old gods, and whether they would then listen to the petty requests of man, for it seemed they often had plans of their own.

Offa had arrived at Ypwinesfloet at high tide on the previous evening, and after a long voyage around the coast he was mightily glad to be back in his homeland. He was hoping for a chance to see the majestic serpents during his stay, but according to reports, no sightings of them had been made in recent weeks. Offa could not believe his eyes when he had first seen the mythical creatures as a child, and they had fascinated him ever since. They were elusive, however, rarely seen in the winter months, and it was definitely getting colder every year, he thought, as he added another log to the fire.

It had been a long time since he had been home. Work on his dyke, separating his kingdom from that of the Welsh, was well underway, and he had been supervising the construction for what now seemed like an age. Having discovered Hadrian's Wall to the north many years ago, he had recognised the man's achievement and the posterity and wealth that gigantic construction had bestowed upon him. Offa too sought fame, and so he had ordered the construction of a western boundary to Mercia, an earthwork that would be called Offa's Dyke, and would be his greatest achievement; ensuring he would become incredibly wealthy and never be forgotten.

His quest for fame had begun long ago. Offa had become fascinated with a book he had been presented with on the day he had become king, and had longed to know the meaning of the strange scribbles contained within the tome. His Christian church advisor had assured him that they were something called words, that spoke of a history regarding the land from the beginning of the Roman era. This concept had intrigued him. He had then demanded to be read the script in full and to hear what the author had written. He listened intently, scoffing at details he knew to be obvious lies, but also entirely missing many critical points of interest. Quickly, though, Offa came to realise that this written record would be all that was left to his people in times to come, and that what was written in those pages would become a truth for the reader, whether the words were genuine or not. That idea had fascinated him too, but Offa did not need to leave a false legacy behind – he had united many kingdoms, created a truly impressive earthwork, built towns and minted his own coinage. He had also sired many children, who were now well placed throughout

Mercia. He was a truly great king with truly great vision; he did not need to pretend to be so.

He sat down by the fire, glad to be home. His Christian tutor would be arriving at any moment to continue his lessons in reading and writing the Latin script. He had not enjoyed being unable to discern the truth of what he was being told was written in the Christian books, and he suspected the cleric was withholding much of what was documented inside them. It was a frustrating language to learn. It seemed incredibly complicated in comparison to his native tongue, but as he always had, he would chip away at the problem day by day, until he had completed his task. He had learned long ago that the gods would always try to help him, but they could only do so much – action with vision would always conquer hope.

Epilogue…

Offa left the world twenty-two years later, in the year 796. He oversaw the completion of work to his dyke, and it remains there as a physical reminder of the incredible power he commanded to this day. Offa was a great king, and when he died, a mighty ship was pulled from the shores of the estuary by Ypwinesfloet to the foot of Offham. Offa was laid within it, alongside all of the riches he would need for the afterlife. Funeral processions went on for many days, and then, as was now becoming a tradition for the great kings of the Anglo-Saxons, a truly mighty mound of earth was constructed over the ship. He lies among his treasures there to this day. He had centred the traditions of the Anglo-Saxons and the future of Britain around that special place, and decades later, it birthed one of the greatest legends of all time…

Beornwulf
Year 827

Chapter - 9

Beornwulf
Year 827

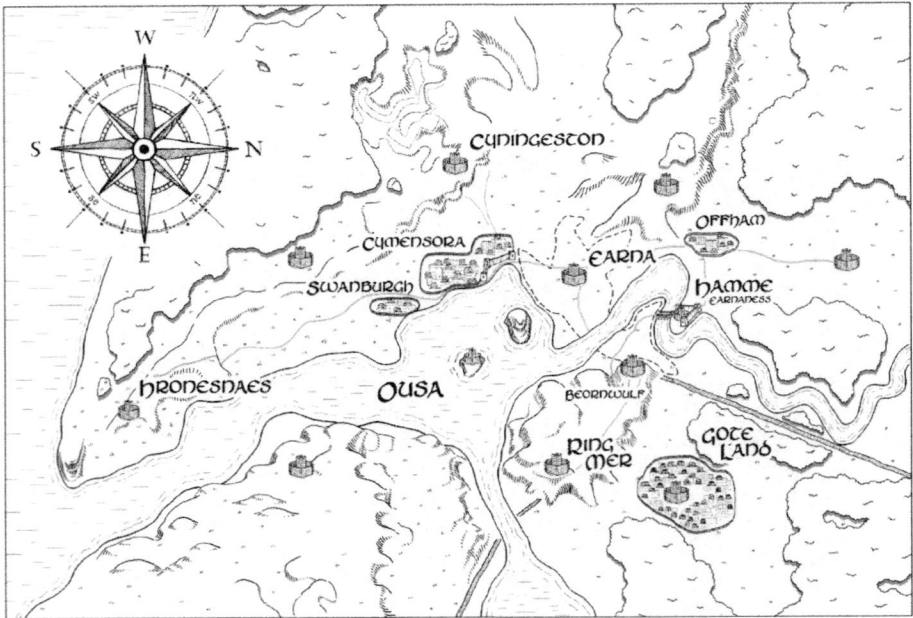

'I think I'm dying, Wiglaf.'

Beo clutched the deep and painful sword wound in his side. He lifted his hand to look once again at the seeping mess between the leather straps of his armour, and winced as he saw it. He knew, deep in his heart, that he would not survive this latest affront to his body. His head sunk low, and he let out a deep sigh of pain and exhaustion.

'Nonsense,' Wiglaf muttered, though in his heart, he too knew it to be true. On many occasions he had seen his king receive far greater wounds than this in battle, yet he had remained as strong as an ox. Never had he seen him brought so low in spirit as this. It worried him greatly. On the journey home from the battlefield, Wiglaf had thought Beo to be suffering the common depression men felt in defeat, but it was more than that, he knew now – Beo's vigour seemed to be waning, and Wiglaf could feel it on him.

'You are Beornwulf, and you will survive!' Wiglaf shouted at him.

But Beo remained silent, his eyes closed, deep in thought. He looked so tired, Wiglaf thought, so very tired. Beo inhaled sharply then blew slowly through his lips, as daggers of pain pulsed through his side once again.

'Not this time, my friend.' He slowly opened his eyes and met Wiglaf's gaze. 'I fear I will not recover as I once did in my youth, Wiglaf. It is my time, dear friend; but truly I did not think my story would end this way. This is not how I wished to die.'

Sadness and a flicker of defeat had crept behind that gaze. Tears formed in Wiglaf's eyes, for he had known nothing but strength from the man seated before him, and seeing the decline in Beornwulf's health broke his tired heart. He sank down to sit beside him on the sturdy wooden bench in the Great Hall, alone for the first time in a week. They had cleared the space so they could speak privately together. In addition to Beornwulf's war wounds, they were both battle-weary and suffering the deep sting of defeat. They had ridden out so confidently against the upstart King Ecgberht just three days past, but the battle had not gone as expected.

Beornwulf stared deeply into the flickering fire, which seemed to spread no heat into the wood-beamed hall inside the wind-battered fortress on the hill. Heavy gusts howled through the timbers ominously, whistling here and there through the small panes of cloudy glass that looked out on to the courtyard. It was a truly grey and miserable day outside, and the scene through the windows reflected well the mood of the surviving warriors as they returned home and filed in slowly through the strong wooden gates, weary and fighting still, against the sucking mud of the thoroughfare.

'This is not how I want to die, Wiglaf!' Beornwulf repeated it louder this time as he drew his gaze from the miserable view. There was anger in his voice now. 'The story of Beornwulf cannot end this way!'

A spark of life returned to his eyes. He stood up too quickly, wincing as the wound opened a little and pain shot through his body. He knew his time was numbered in days now, maybe even in hours, he thought; he had never felt this weak before. He had suffered wounds like this in the past, but this one felt different. A poison seemed to be creeping into the incision, and trailing veins of blackness were beginning to spider out from its edges.

'Help me with my armour, my friend. I feel the weight of it increasing on me by the hour.'

Wiglaf stood and unbuckled the shoulder straps, gently easing off the shoulder plates and pulling the chainmail hauberk carefully over Beo's head. With the heavy armour removed, Beo began to feel a little forgotten strength returning to his limbs, and a new determination began to surface within him. He had made his decision.

'I fear I do not have long, Wiglaf, and I will not let my story end here in defeat. Not here, and not from a mere babe's sword wound, no less. Nay,

Wiglaf, I cannot let it be thus, so I swear by all that I hold dear that from this moment forward, my mind shall be set to one task only. I will go to face the dreaded serpent that plagues our people, and I will do so this very hour, before my life leaves me entirely. With what is left of my dying strength, I will attempt to rid our lands of this creature's wrath, and I thank the gods for this final chance at glory against a foe such as he, for without him, I would surely die defeated!'

The boast sounded heartfelt. Wiglaf's sunken eyes brightened a little and a small smile evidenced the glimmer of hope sparking deep within him. Beo was back!

Wiglaf had not thought of the Dragon in months now, it seemed. The beast had been quiet in the last year, and rare was a sighting of him reported in recent days, but the people of the land were in terror of him still. Wiglaf thought back to the destruction that had been dealt them on that terrible night, two winters past...

Fire had fallen from the sky in that year, and five of the seven hilltop forts had been badly damaged – three had been razed to the ground. Farmhouses and many people of the land were consumed in flame as the fiery rock rained down without mercy. Over the subsequent days, cattle were found dead from sheer terror. Many had drowned in the estuary as they tried to flee the inescapable attack from the heavens. Fortunately. some remained alive, but most were scattered across the hills and food was short that year. The slow and arduous labour required to reconstruct the forts had then taken its toll on the people and left the land vulnerable to attack from the merciless Vikings, who had sent many raiding parties over the seas in the following months. The first attacks were thwarted quickly by Beo and his warriors, who hung the butchered Vikings from a scaffold on their hilltop, leaving an ugly warning for all future raiders to see as they sailed up the

Ouosa seeking plunder. The message was clear; the Anglo-Saxon kings would not be defeated so easily.

Those seven hilltop forts in Sussex had kept that land safe for generations, and now the banded kings of the Anglo-Saxons had been forced to defend the land without them, and, at the same time, reconstruct their defensive structures in as short a time as possible. It had left the kingdom weakened, and the people hated the serpent for that. In truth, not a soul had actually seen the beast launching the fireballs from the heavens on that fateful night, but they had become convinced it was he, and as the stories were told and retold, this possibility became a fact. It was the serpent's wrath brought upon them, he whose home steamed with fiery vapours from deep within the earth, vengeance for the killing of his kinsfolk, they murmured. Retribution for the theft of the precious vessel that had long lain within that steaming mound.

Wiglaf saw some fire was now coming back to Beo's eyes, and his heart sang. This was the king he knew and loved; this was the man he had followed into hell and, every time, this was the man who had led him safely home. The giant warrior who willingly chose to do what all others would not, and who Wiglaf would follow to the ends of the earth to be with him as he did so. He was his friend, who he admired above all others.

'I fear I do not have long before my strength will no longer be sufficient for the task at hand, Wiglaf, but win or lose, I must go to face my end in battle and attempt to rid our people of this cave-dwelling serpent that has terrorised us for too long now. Perhaps some good may still be done before my passing.'

He picked up his shield and tested his arm's ability to hold it above the wound in his side. His nerves shrieked with pain as he did so, but

Beornwulf steadied himself and cleared his mind of the agony. While there was breath left in his body, he vowed, he would not be brought down by mere discomfort. He lifted his sword, and found his right arm was still quite capable of hefting the short, sharp blade. It was only when he swung with too much vigour that the searing pain flared up within him. He tested it once again and found himself well capable of delivering a powerful strike.

Beornwulf had quickly broken every sword he had ever owned; this one, however, was shorter and broader than any he had ever had in his possession. After consistently shattering every sword built for smaller, weaker men, he had taken it upon himself to design and forge a blade of his own; a blade that would not shatter from the force of a man as powerful as he. For Beornwulf was indeed a big man; over six foot seven and heavily built. He towered above his kinsfolk, and only once in his life had he and his warriors seen another man as big as he. It was on a legendary trip to Denmark many years past to aid King Hrothgar that Beo had battled with him. Grendel, the wild beast-man came to be known as, and when they clashed together in the great hall, wrestling hand to hand, it was recounted to have been like watching the old gods fighting. Beornwulf had grown a loyal following since that day. His people thought it likely that he was a descendant of the ancient Giant Kings that had roamed these parts in ages past, and perhaps they were correct; a man of his size and stature was rare in those days. His people had seen the possibility of greatness in the child Beornwulf long before he had become king, and with a man like him as their leader, none had dared to attack their hilltop stronghold in living memory; but those days, it seemed, were coming to an end.

Wiglaf stood and reached for his greatcoat to protect himself from the brutal weather howling at the door. Beo stayed his arm and met his eyes.

'Wiglaf, this is not a task for you, my friend, nor is it the task of any man save me alone to go and meet my fate as I must this day. Live on, my friend, live on and tell tall tales of our adventures!'

Wiglaf's eyes narrowed as he spoke. 'You know I will not let you do this alone, dear Beo, for I would rather join you on one last adventure and test my mettle alongside you as I have in all our years of brotherhood than live a day more on this earth having abandoned you at the last!'

They grinned at each other. Strength in friendship flowed between them, and excitement began to build for their final adventure. They grasped hands with a fierce grip, then clashed and ground their heads together in a Saxon warriors' pact.

Beo sheathed his sword and patted the hilt of his dagger to make sure it was still in its scabbard. He hefted his shield, swung it on to his back and, with a mutual nod of readiness between them, Beo left his home for the last time without a backward glance. Ignoring his agony and the quizzical glances from his warriors, he strode boldly through the courtyard eager to meet his fate, his head held high, but his heart hammering with a sensation he had not experienced often. He knew that this sensation was fear, and he was unaccustomed to it. It was undoubtedly a deep fear of the serpent, of the strange unknown monster that hid beneath the burial mound. There was also a fear of the wound that seemed to be quickly stealing the life away from him, but above both of these things there was a fear of dying with the sting of defeat in his bones, and that was something he would not allow. Time was not on his side, but he was determined his story would be sung loudly and proudly by his people after he died. Beornwulf would go out fighting for his last breath, fighting for his people, fighting to leave this life victorious, exactly as he had lived it.

They trudged on through the gates and began their march towards the serpent's lair at the foot of the Eagle's Head; the place where Beornwulf would meet his fate with a blade in his hand, fighting unto his last. Eleven of his most loyal warriors followed after them, without hesitation and without so much as a question.

So went they, thirteen men exiting the gates of the wooden fortress high above Gote farm, 'the farm of the Geats', beneath the enormous downland escarpment known as Ring Mer, or 'the great hill ring, surrounded by the sea'. The wind began to whip mercilessly at them as they left the protection of the fortress walls. Rarely did a day go by on that high hill bluff that the wind did not blow heavy and hard, and for this reason, and because of their great love of sailing, the Anglo-Saxon hill-fort people had come to be known as the wind-loving folk. The warriors narrowed their eyes as the drizzle lashed hard at their faces. They were barely able to see the path in front of them; but were so familiar with the land - that they made their way with ease towards the steep sloping valley that led down to Maulling and Ypwinesfloet. That special place was one of Beornwulf's ancestors' first settlements; he had made good use of the well-built port and villa buildings left behind by the Romans there as they exited Britain some four hundred years past. So long ago were those Romans here, and so prolific was their construction work, far surpassing the Saxon builders' abilities, that the local folk now whispered that giants had constructed the buildings and the port walls with their impossible, arched stonework, but Beornwulf knew better. They had held many important Witans at the church on the promontory in years past, and he knew the history of the area well.

In a short time they had reached the foot of the valley, and made their way towards the stone wall and the magnificently constructed bridge that crossed over the Ousa at the foot of the Eagle, connecting Maulling to Hamme and Offham. Beornwulf had always assumed that the Romans had built this enormous wall and bridge to defend their people, who it seemed had come here to settle along the edges of the tidal estuary, and also by the rivers of the Midwinde which flowed back into the furthest reaches of the Ousa inland. The remains of the Roman villas were still present there, with their strangely tiled floors and stone walls, but the Anglo-Saxons had not attempted to rebuild them as they fell into disrepair. They were a people who preferred to live in homes made of timber; they were proficient woodworkers, and so had continued to build in this way. The hard, raised stone floors had proved useful as a footing for their own buildings, but as the population increased, the preformed Roman platforms for their homes had quickly been repurposed, and none were left to utilise now.

Beornwulf strode boldly across the bridge to Hamme and saw the beautiful church of St Peter he had helped to construct standing proud atop the great mound, the abandoned seat of nobility. His heart began to thump loudly in his chest. No one had approached this promontory of the mainland in many years. So full of burial mounds and ancient tombs was it that the local people were sure it was a haunted place, and since the Dragon had been discovered occupying this piece of land, the local populace had avoided it for many years. It was here, though, below the church, on the far side of the promontory, and at the foot of the steep scree and dirt slope, that the entrance to the serpent's lair was to be found. A stream flowed out from that place through an arched opening at the foot of the rise; the sulphurous water there was vaporous and hot. Beornwulf knew of many such springs across the downlands, but this one alone flowed out from beneath the mound, emerging as a deep stream which flowed into the sand of the sea estuary.

The men stood together on the wall of the promontory above the flowing stream below, their eyes seeking fearfully for any sign of the serpent in the waters, but they saw nothing. Clearly, the beast was hiding in his lair amongst his ancient treasures.

Beornwulf turned to his men and saw the raw terror in their eyes. He too was afraid, but he would not let fear hold him back as it did so many others. He gathered his courage, and addressed them for the last time.

'Wait now on this hill, clad in your corslets, my warriors of great renown. This is not a task for you, nor is it within the measure of any man save me alone to go and face this dread serpent, as I must this day. I will slay it or die trying, and in victory or defeat, I fear that this time I will not return. Live well, die brave, my friends.'

With those parting words, he lit his torch, strode boldly down the slope and stepped purposefully into the hot, reeking stream. Adrenaline began to course through his blood as Beo waded his way to the centre of the wall, whence the hot waters flowed. It was up to his armpits now, and he knew that if it got any deeper he would not be able to continue. With a heavy sword and shield, swimming here would be impossible. Soon enough, though, he stood at the arched stone entrance to the lair and could no longer see his men above him. He licked his dry lips nervously. Never had he been so afraid. Now screamed he, a challenge down the dark, dank tunnel to raise courage from within his heart, and deep under the earth, he heard movement. A clinking of metal on metal. His pulse quickened further, but his resolve grew stronger. It was time to meet his fate.

Beo ducked his head under the arch and slowly waded on under the promontory. The water was becoming slightly shallower here, and thankfully – he was able to hold his sword above the waist-deep reek. His half-submerged shield pushed a small wake in front of him, his arm held fast through the handle loops, allowing him to grip the torch with his free hand.

His eyes widened as he sensed a change in the motion of the steaming water ahead of him. Something was moving towards him. Beo screamed

a war-cry once more to gain courage, planted his feet in the slimy bed of the stream and then, through the glow of the torch, he saw the thing coming at him through the water, winding and sliding, snakelike on the surface. It was roughly ten feet in length, with tough, silver-scaled skin covering its entire body, and Beo saw a look of menace in its cold black eyes.

Silently and with a dreadful purpose it came, and terror began to flood Beo's veins. Suddenly, he was not so sure of himself, but it was too late — the fight was upon him.

The beast's head reared up from the water and slammed into his shield. It held, but the creature was enraged and came at him again, its serpent tongue flicking at the air before the giant mouth opened and bit down hard on top of the shield's iron rim once more. Beo drew back his right arm and stabbed his sword forward, around the side of his shield. The blade slid off the serpent's side with no effect, but he did not have room to swing the sword overhead in the small tunnel. He was now panicked, and uncertain of how he could inflict a death blow.

Above him, on the wall of the promontory, Wiglaf heard the struggle below and shame filled his heart. He hesitated not. Drawing his sword, he ran to his friend's aid as fast as his legs would carry him, while below the earth, Beornwulf fought on, slowly giving ground, as the beast pushed him back towards the entrance to his underground lair.

He stepped into the stream and waded fast to Beornwulf's aid. He could hear the struggle now, and he bellowed as loud as his voice was able.

'Go on, dear Beornwulf, and do what you said you'd do when you were young and full of vigour. Now must you, brave in deeds, your heart unwavering, with all your might, thy life defend! To the last, I will aid you, my friend!'

Strength from support flowed into Beornwulf's veins, and ignoring the life slowly stealing away from him, he fought on with renewed determination.

Wiglaf joined the assault as Beornwulf and the beast emerged from the tunnel back into the daylight. He did not have time to take in what he was witnessing, and it was not his wont to hesitate in times of battle. Heaving his sword high, he drove it down with all his might, and his blade connected hard with the serpent's head. Enraged as pain shot through its body, it rose up once again and crashed down hard, its mighty jaws sinking into Beo's shield and the flesh of his shoulder and neck, but Beo did not hesitate for a second in his agonies; he saw his opportunity as the beast was locked upon him. Dropping his sword in the reeking waters, he drew his razor-edged dagger from its sheath and drove it upwards from beneath him with all the strength he had left to offer. The sharp knife sunk deeply into the beast's softer underbelly, and Beo saw a spasm of pain and fear flare in its eyes as the blade pierced its vital organs. The beast's strength was stolen quickly away from it then; the force of its jaws on his shield and his shoulder easing off, as the light of life dimmed slowly inside the mighty creature's eyes. As it released its grip and sank slowly to the bed of the stream, blood gushed forth from Beo's new wound, his mind clouded over, and he slipped into the black chasm of unconsciousness. Wiglaf caught him in his arms, and heaved Beo's enormous frame from the bloodied waters.

Beornwulf awoke to find himself propped up against the stone port wall. As his eyes began to clear, he saw to his left the enormous Roman arches, held aloft by vast stone pillars, and he marvelled at their construction. His vision was blurring and a hot, searing pain enveloped his neck and shoulder, issuing forth from where the serpent had bitten him. He then remembered what he had done. He had killed the Dragon! Through his death pains, he managed a small smile. He would die victorious. And with that thought, the great agony began to ease inside him.

'Beo, Beo, Beo!'

Beornwulf became aware of Wiglaf shouting at him, while he sprinkled cold water on to his face and neck to wake him. Their eyes met again, and through his streaming tears of sadness, Wiglaf's face lit up with joy.

'I thought I had lost you, dear Beo!' he exclaimed as he wiped his tears away with the back of his sleeve.

Beo grinned at him, but it was with all the strength he could muster that he did so. 'I do not have long, Wiglaf my friend, and before my passing, I would make this request of you; go swiftly now and look upon that long-hoarded wealth beneath the ground. I should like to see more of these mighty heirlooms we have won with our strength in will. More peaceful will my passing be were I to know I leave my people well furnished with gold and wealth to aid them in their futures.'

Wiglaf heeded his friend's request. He knew that time was short, so without delay he lit his abandoned torch, ran back into the stinking hot waters, past the seat of nobility above him, and under the earth he went. Deep underground, he emerged from the tunnel into a large pool and with eyes filled with wonder, he saw he was inside a square structure with magnificent columns supporting the roof. Stacked against the walkway that surrounded the pool were golden treasures and jewels beyond measure. Rusted helms and ancient armour hung neatly on the walls. He saw ewers and vessels, all made of gold and caked in jewels, their fair adornment slowly disintegrating in the ceaseless march of time. Then hanging there, in a small room adjoining the walkway surrounding the chamber, his torch reflected beautiful light on a mighty banner, all made of gold, that cast a luminous glow on to the scene beneath it.

Wiglaf remembered his mission. Quickly, he gathered the best of what he could see before him. All that he could carry he gathered about him, then hastened back to Beornwulf's side. He did not know if he would find him alive still, and the thought urged him on faster through the steaming stream. He came to Beo's resting place once again, dropping those ancient treasures as he did so to seize upon the true treasure of his life, his king and his friend. Beornwulf's eyes were closed, and once again, fear and sadness began to well up within Wiglaf's heart.

'Beo! Beo! Beo!'

He shook his arms gently again, and Beo's eyes jerked back to consciousness for the very last time. His body seemed incapable of movement now, but speech burst forth from his breast, and Wiglaf listened hard to his greatest friend's departing words.

'To you, Wiglaf, and to the everlasting Lord, most glorious king and master of all, I offer my thanks for these fair treasures I now gaze upon. I bartered my life for those precious things, so that in my passing I might ask of you to use that gold to care for my people's needs. No longer may I here remain. Bid my men, renowned in war, to build a mound for me when the pyre is done. It should tower on high upon Hronesnaes as a memorial to my folk. Build it high, Wiglaf, so even they who sail their ships over the shadows of the deep will point and exclaim that there be Beornwulf's barrow, and they will remember me.'

Beo gathered the last of the life within him. In great pain, he removed the golden torque from around his neck, then the golden ring of kingship from his finger, and presented them to Wiglaf.

'My brother, you are the last of the house of Waegmund's line. All hath fate swept away at their appointed time. I must follow them!'

And with those words, Beo's eyes closed for the last time, his hands opened skyward, and his soul departed from his body, hastening forth to take its rightful place amongst the steadfast ones.

Wiglaf's sorrow was plain to see when the remaining warriors came down from the bluff to meet him. Grief flooded his being, and it was all he could do not to berate those men for leaving their king to die alone. He had witnessed the fear and lack of will in them, plain to see when he had departed to aid his friend against the serpent. But he remembered that Beo had asked them to remain there, and they had done his bidding. A little more willingly, perhaps, than Wiglaf would have hoped. These were the men that were left for him to help guard this land; he saw weakness in them now, and he began to worry for the future of his people.

Together, they built a strong bier for Beornwulf and laid him upon it with a great amount of treasure they had now long looted from the vault. No small amount of gold would go up with him in the hot surging fires of his funeral pyre.

When all was made ready, the twelve men lifted him atop their shoulders and began the long march along the Swan road to Titlescomb, following the well-established processional route through Kings Town where Hrethel ruled, then onward to the ancient burial grounds on the hilltops by Hronesnaes.

The land fell silent as they departed it. The Dragon was now dead, but it would take many years for fear of that place to leave the unconscious memory of man.

Epilogue…

War fell on the populace in the months following Beornwulf's death. King Ecgberth of Wessex was only a child when he had been forced into exile by the Viking invaders Offa and Beohtric. As he had grown into a man, they had slowly conquered and stolen his ancestral lands from him, forcing him to seek sanctuary in the land of the Franks.

Many years later, Beohtric died and left the throne of Wessex empty once again. Ecgberth garnered significant support from the Franks and returned home to reclaim his rightful place as the King of Wessex. The skirmishes were brief. He re-took the greater part of his lands quickly, but the kingdom of the South Saxons would not bend the knee so easily. However, in King Ecgberth's final battle, he defeated the pagan Saxons and drove out King Wiglaf from Wessex. Ecgberth then installed his own vassal King, Ludecan, in his place, but his victory was short-lived. In the same year, fuelled by a defeat he would not let stand, Wiglaf returned to Britain with the mightiest army he could muster from his ancestral lands in Sweden. A great and bloody battle ensued as they approached their home on the high hill by Ypwinesfloet. Aethelwulf, son of Ecgberth, had been warned of the Saxon army which had landed on the shores of Pevensey and had gathered the largest force he could summon to face them. They met in a valley beneath the hills of Sussex, and the battle raged on for most of the day. Thousands of great warriors on both sides of the lines died that day, and the rivers ran red with blood. Thereafter, the battlefield was ever known as 'Terrible Down'.

Wiglaf fought hard that day, and won back his lands in a victory that left the army of Ecgberth greatly depleted for many years. He held his lands fast for his people from that day forward, and conquered much of Britain. Wiglaf became known as a great Anglo-Saxon king, who reigned well until the end of his days. His people honoured him when he died and, at his request, they buried him in a barrow on the high hills of Hronesnaes, beside the man he had admired the most.

Soon after, another great king was birthed in those lands. He began his rise to the throne fighting relentless Viking invasions. He fought hard for Christianity, yet he very nearly lost the entire island of Britain to the fierce Saxon raiders; but as with all great men, he rose from the swamps and became remembered as one of the greatest men in history. After many years of struggle, and an unlikely friendship with an influential Viking lord, he negotiated a way to peace with the pagan Saxons. His name was Alfred the Great.

Alfred took over Ypwinesfloet and the ancestral birthing grounds of Christianity in Britain. The people there accepted his rule willingly. Remnants of many nations were alive in that place, and Alfred tried hard to accept, unite and Christianise them all. He forged Wessex's capital in Laewes, utilising the well-known location to meet with many kings and queens in the surrounding realms and he established two mints to further the importance of the area.

Alfred became a learned scribe and began to write many documents in his later years. Before his death and succession by Aethelstan, he attempted to pen the history of the land in as much detail as was available to him. It was one of his greatest works, and came to be known as 'The Anglo-Saxon Chronicle'. But the story he copied down most joyfully, orated to him by an old Viking warrior in his dying years, is the story that would become famous throughout the world. That epic tale was called 'Beowulf'.

Aethelstan
Year 925

Aethelstan
Year 925

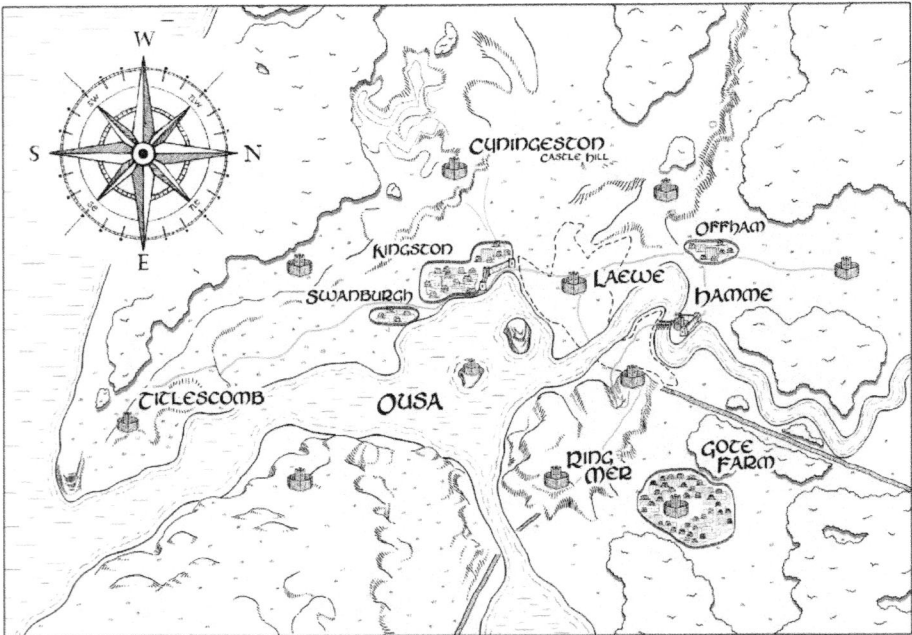

Aethelstan stared at the assembled mass of great men and women who stood before him. The anointing oil had been applied. The Archbishop of Canterbury finished his rites, reverently placed the golden crown on Aethelstan's head, then stepped from the dais and addressed the crowd.

'All hail King Aethelstan!' he cried, as he moved to his side and presented the new king.

'All hail King Aethelstan!' the crowd chorused back. They sank to their knees, bowing their heads in respect.

Aethelstan spoke loudly as he stood. 'Rise, my people. Rise! I would not have you great men and women on your knees before me; we are now united as brothers and sisters!' He shouted the last, sweeping his hands upwards and smiling broadly at the people gathered before him.

The crowd rose together, roaring their approval for their new king. He took in the scene before him. Aethelstan was filled with a joy he had not experienced until this day. After many years of battle, hardship, and a great amount of work, he had finally succeeded. Though none had believed it possible, he had found a lasting way to peace with the invading Swedes, Franks and Danes.

Aethelstan had arranged and administered his sister's marriage to Otho, king of the ruling family of the South Saxons, in this very church in Kingston just two years past. This had united the Saxons to his cause by blood. The history of his and their people had been forged in these lands, and Aethelstan was fully aware of the great legends that had been birthed here. He knew of the tombs beneath St Peter's Church and of the great treasures and remarkable people that rested in those vaults, and because of this, his faith was unshakable. Like Alfred before him, he did not need faith – he knew.

That holy site was so important to him that Aethelstan had held many of his most critical Witans there. The church was perfectly positioned for kings and queens from neighbouring lands to reach easily by boat and, as far as he was concerned, it was the centre point of English history. The meeting place was known as Clofesho to outsiders, but to Aethelstan it was 'Hamme' (Home). He felt at his strongest there. He had now united the Saxon people's leaders with his own family, and they had at last accepted his position as Rex totius Britanniae – King of all Britain. The cheers continued unabated, until Aethelstan waved them all slowly to silence.

'Let us feast, and celebrate our new alliance,' he shouted. 'Together, we will fight to secure our country under one cause; we will fight for unity!' He had chosen his words carefully. The Danes and Swedes were proud people, who lived for war, adventure and glory, and he would use those qualities to his best advantage. Besides which, if they were not engaged to his purpose, he was certain that they would soon begin warring with each other once again.

The crowd roared their approval, and stewards began to usher the masses from the great wooden church at the foot of Castle Hill into the courtyard within the fortification the South Saxons had once called Cymensora, but was now known simply as Kingston. It was a beautiful day beyond those sturdy oak doors. The colours of late autumn rippled on the trees as a gentle breeze ruffled the fine flags of many nations, pinned to poles set high above the vast array of tents in the farm of the kings. Below the church on the small rise, a glorious array of dishes and gifts from many nations had been assembled for the royal feast. Aethelstan too had many fine gifts of his own to bestow upon his new vassals.

The celebrations continued late into the evening. Braziers were lit. Music from far-off lands, and in many languages, was performed joyously and enjoyed by all. An atmosphere of proud cultural expression ensued, with unique dances, drinking games and competitions. Great revelry was had that evening as the mead flowed heavily. Hunting dogs, horses and weaponry were admired and compared while people celebrated a new experience of mixed cultural interest, peace and festivity. Many strong bonds of friendship were forged by the leaders of many countries that day.

Epilogue...

Two years after his coronation, Aethelstan faced fierce resistance from the Celtic nations. Rumours came to him of a mighty fleet of ships gathering to the north of Ireland. Olaf Guthfrithson, King of Dublin, had forged an alliance with Constantine of the Scots and Owain of Strathclyde. He was summoning great warriors to his cause to take revenge on the English for their many years of pride and arrogance. Scots, Vikings, Welsh, Irish, Cornish and Cumbrians flocked to his banner. Olaf set sail with a fleet of six hundred and fifteen ships and landed on the coast of Northumbria at the mouth of the Humber. Heavily overpowered, the Northumbrians put up little resistance.

Aethelstan and his army rode north to face them. Outnumbered, but now with a battle-hardened, well-tested army of fierce Viking warriors of his own, along with veteran Mercians and West Saxons, the two armies met on even ground. Aethelstan called on the blessings of God, and attacked the vastly superior invading forces at Brunanburh. His charge of heavy horse and his well-seasoned warriors fought like men possessed, butchering then routing the Celtic forces in a decisive victory that would shape the very future of the British Isles. It was one of the most critical battles of English history.

Hugh de Payens
Year 1133

Chapter - 11

Hugh de Payens
Year 1133

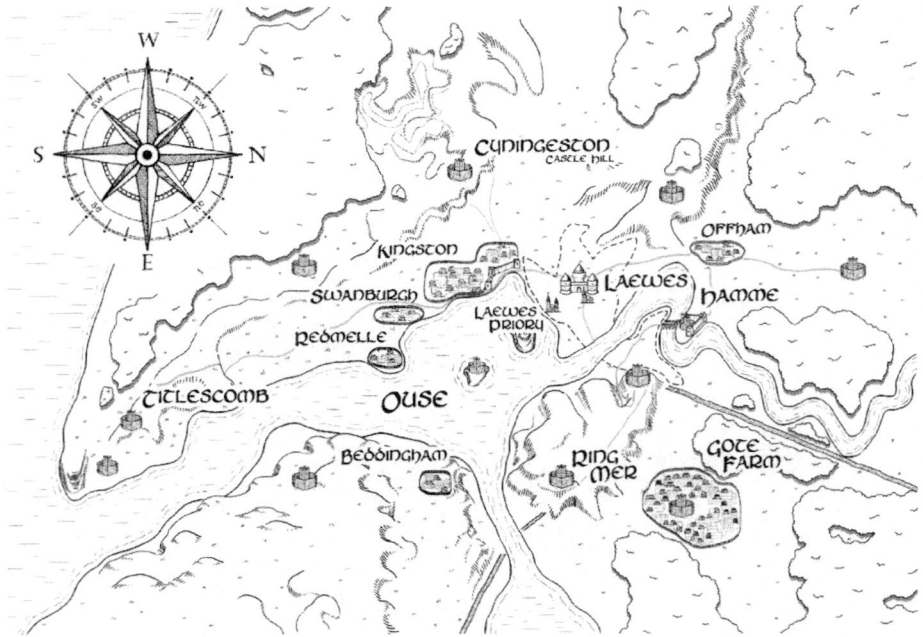

The Grand Master exited the fortifications at Hamme. The gateway had opened, and Hugues stepped through into a world of confusion. The multitude of gathered numbers outside was far beyond his wildest dreams. They had come as requested. The Templars had worked hard to send messengers into faraway lands in a drive to recruit strong men to their order, and now hundreds of brave souls had arrived to attempt to join their ranks. He had little doubt that the gathered folk had heard the fine tales of heroism and bravery from his knights as they protected the route to the Holy Land, but he had not expected so much support this day, though he was glad of it; the Templars needed many brave new recruits.

It was a mighty long pilgrimage from Sussex to Jerusalem, and that perilous route had come under attack many times before the Knights' formation, but since they had banded together, the road had become well protected; passage was now safer than it had been since the age of the Romans. Trade had begun to flourish along the route, and people had donated great wealth to the order to continue their work. They were becoming very powerful, and Hugues was now in Britain to attempt to swell the Templars' ranks and land-holdings. He had spent the evening in a local tavern, the Turk's Head in Lewes, before retiring to the Church of the Holy Sepulchre. The local patrons had gawked at the mailed knight sitting quietly in the corner of the inn, drinking only water. Quickly, they too had spread word of his presence in the town, but he had never imagined so many men would come this day, and he wondered now what in the heavens he was going to do with them all.

Hugues understood clearly that the majority of the people gathered before him were simply looking for a free meal. Most were unfit to join the order, and he now needed to thin the herd and see what he was left with. He took control of the situation, organising strength and health tests, quickly dismissing anybody who fell short of the basic requirements. This immediately cut the numbers in half. Next, he called upon any recruits with living families they wished to see again and, once they had gathered together, he dismissed them too. Now he was left with less than half the number again. He lined up the remaining men and examined them intently one by one, and at the last, he stared deeply into their eyes to measure their courage. He said nothing as he did so, but after this unnerving scrutiny, he called forward nine of the twenty-one men and dismissed them as well. The remaining twelve would now be given the uniform of an initiate and undertake their training. If any of them were found wanting in mind, body or spirit, they too would be dismissed, but if they made it through the arduous testing and instruction, they would have the great honour of becoming Sergeants in the Templar Order. They would then gain all of the benefits and respect associated with that rank. It was the highest position that these men could aim for within the Order; full Knighthood could only be granted to men of distinguished lineage, and these lads were peasants.

Hugues presented them their white cloaks, to the cheers of the crowd, then ordered them to follow him. Together, they began the short journey to the Church of the Holy Sepulchre at the foot of the town, on Albion Street. The sun was at its zenith. It was unbearably hot, and Hugues felt lightheaded in his full chain mail and armour, but he had survived far harsher conditions in the Holy Land and he would not show a hint of weakness to these new recruits; standards had to be set for these men, and Hugues de Payens was the right man for the job.

They followed the trackway back to the town at a fast pace, Hugues eager to find some shade and to break his fast. Marching along the thin trail, they noticed a small group of women cleaning pelts in one of the cold-water springs near the church. The new recruits stole some quick glances towards them, feeling proud in their regalia and hoping for some admiration for their new status, but the women barely noticed them.

'Eyes forward!' Hugues bellowed. The recruits snapped their attention back to Hugues as he strode purposefully up the small rise to the church ahead of them.

'How had he known?' they all wondered. He was not even looking their way.

'The time for seeking women is now over,' he shouted. 'As novices, you will be required to live by your vows, and, as well you know, we are a celibate Order. Your seed, young men, is your hidden power; you must conserve it at all costs. If you are not yet ready to live this life, you are still free to depart, but I warn you; once you have sworn your oaths, you will be held to every vow you make to us.' He stopped and turned to face them.

Somewhat chastened at their immediate and obvious lack of control, they bowed their heads in apology, and Hugues nodded his acceptance.

'Come then,' he stated. 'Let us begin to make powerful men of you.'

Godefroy de St Omer welcomed Hugues and the new recruits in as they arrived back at the church. He was a large and fierce-looking man, with startling blue eyes that seemed to penetrate the soul. The new recruits were both impressed and suitably cowed by the man's great frame, piercing eyes and thick black beard. They walked into the courtyard and looked around with wide eyes. No man but a Templar could enter this place, and it had grown an aura of whispered mystery about it among the local townsfolk. There was nothing particularly remarkable about the expansive buildings and church, it now seemed, but the site was steeped in history and the initiates were suitably enthralled by their new home. Godefroy led them to their lodgings. They would be in shared quarters, and he gestured for them to enter a large, cold and sparsely furnished room. It was simple, but had been kept spotlessly clean.

'Settle yourselves in,' Godefroy instructed. 'No talking. We will be back to get you shortly. Once you have taken your first vows, we will cut your hair, then you will scrub yourselves clean. You will then receive the black undergarments of an initiate, a padded jerkin and your practice sword. You will treat your lodgings and your equipment with the utmost respect and care. From this moment on, any lapse in attention may cost you or your brothers your life, so listen well to your first lessons. The time for childish games is over. The time of Knighthood begins.'

Godefroy left the young men behind and went to speak with Hugues. He found him in the kitchens, eating some simple bread and a terribly thin vegetable broth.

'Lord, this stew could use some meat in it!' Hugues complained. 'Is this your doing?' He picked up a spoonful and dribbled it back into the bowl, a look of great distaste on his face.

'You know the rules, Hugues,' Godefroy chuckled. He deepened his voice and waggled his finger in an excellent imitation of their old Cistercian teacher. 'Too much meat weakens the body, and corrupts the soul,' he mimicked.

'Yes, yes,' Hugues replied tiredly, a smile forming on his face. 'But surely you can do better than this?'

Godefroy laughed heartily. 'You always were a great complainer, Hugues, but it is good to see you back, brother. I feel I must thank you again for securing the new donations to the vaults in my stead.'

Hugues waved away his concern. 'Do not fret, Godefroy. I know how that place disturbs your peace. There is a strange atmosphere down there, it is true, and the secrets it holds would make any man uneasy, but with your family connection to the exiled king who lies there, I do not blame you for wanting to stay away from it.'

Godefroy nodded. 'Aye. A confusion of memory afflicts me in that space, and I lose track of my place in time. The concerns of Dagobert II are no longer the concern of the Omer family, yet my blood is called to action in that place.'

Hugues nodded his head as he swallowed another mouthful of wetted bread. 'Well, do not concern yourself, brother; the funds are safely deposited in the vaults and the credit notes have now been signed and granted to the pilgrims by our Sergeants there. All is well below the church and the entrance is well secured. We have nothing to fear, Godefroy; the Saye family are very capable, it would seem.'

'That is good news, brother. It is hard to believe how much wealth has begun to gather in our vaults now, is it not? It only seems like yesterday we were penniless and sharing a bow-backed horse on our way to the Holy Land.'

'We have come a long way, there's no denying it,' Hugues agreed. 'But we still have much to accomplish. The road to Jerusalem is long, and we need an army of capable Sergeants to protect it. These boys are all uneducated, untested and weak. It is truly shocking, brother, but they were the best of the lot. We have our work cut out for us, Godefroy, so we had better get started.'

Epilogue…

Hugues de Payens died on the island of Bornholm three years later. He was pursuing a mystery that had confounded him since his first visit beneath the church of St Peter, to which he never found the answer. As he scoured the land and explored the caves there, he became very ill. Crippling chest pains and a terrible fever racked his body. The local inhabitants had seen the disease before, and referred to the painful illness as 'the grip of the phantom'. Hugues died of the mysterious malady in mere days, and was buried on Bornholm shortly thereafter.

The Templar Order remained present on Britain's southern shores and grew exponentially in power, influence and wealth. Royal families across the world now attempted to utilise the Knights for their own political ends and for fear that the Order of the Temple of Solomon would one day supersede their own authority. They tried hard to keep well informed regarding their activities, but with such mighty support from the church in Rome, there was little anyone could do to stop them. The Templars gathered untold fortunes for the church, and gained a fierce reputation. Monarchies across the known world had little choice but to accede to the pope and his mighty army of knights; they still held power in their own lands, but the Templars were not to be underestimated. They had assumed much unwanted authority, but despite their overreach, the lords and rulers of many nations were too cowed by their legend and prowess to confront them. But not all of the barons would lie down without a fight…

William de Saye III
Year 1264

Chapter - 12

William de Saye III
Year 1264

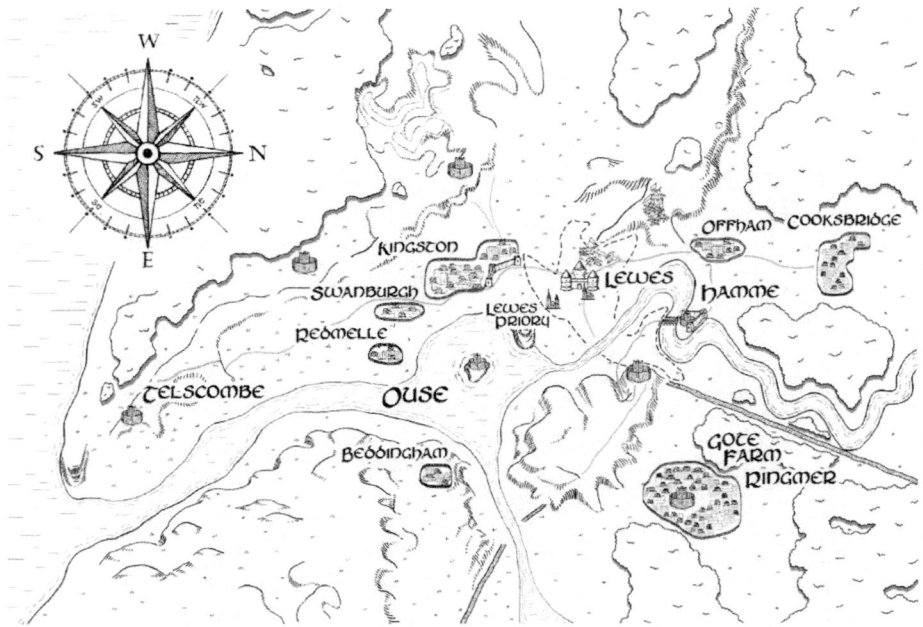

William's knee ached under the weight of his Templar armour as he strode up the main thoroughfare towards Lewes Castle. His recent, third pilgrimage to the Holy Land had taken its toll on his health, but his duties were irritatingly unavoidable. He was on his way to meet with the utter halfwit the country now called King.

Much to Williams's dismay, and despite the Templars' great influence and power, the Pope still needed the allegiance of the monarchies of the world to control the populace of each nation, but it was common knowledge that the English king was a fool. Henry III had so far managed to achieve absolutely nothing of note during his long reign. He had, however, managed to slowly lose control of his country, piece by undeniable piece, and the usurper baron, Simon de Montfort, had taken full advantage of his idiocy. Simon had recognised the king for the inbred fool that he was, and had seen his opportunity to utilise him as a puppet from their very first meeting. He had insinuated himself into the court and suffered Henry's company for many years until the king truly believed himself unable to run the country without him. Simon had then secretly married Henry's sister, spent vast amounts of money he had assured his lenders were guaranteed by the crown and incredibly, Henry had known nothing about it. Any other king would have executed the turncoat on discovering this outrage, thought William, but Henry had forgiven Montfort, paid his debts and, under the advice of his court, simply banished him from his presence. The sad truth was that, even after all of that, Henry had still not wanted to let him go. He had truly believed Simon to be a firm and honourable friend, but Montfort was ambitious and unhappy with the current state of the country. He had manipulated the king with consummate ease, slowly attempting to steal away his power. Everyone had seen this clearly, but the king had been blind to Montfort's lies. Now, however, angry and betrayed, the king was at last under no illusion. He had just received disturbing news; Simon and the disgruntled barons were on their way to attack Henry at Lewes Castle with a mighty army at their back. Simon now wanted total control handed over to himself, and his new government. The king was in deep trouble; he had no aptitude for warfare – he had no aptitude for much at all really – so as he always did, he had called on William to make the tough decisions for him.

William entered the forecourt to the castle. It never failed to impress him. Built some two centuries past out of flint and mortar, Lewes Castle soared high above the town, providing stunning views of the surrounding countryside. It was one of the safest fortifications in the south of England. William Warenne had been granted the old wooden fort and the surrounding lands by William the Conqueror after his decisive victory at the battle of Hastings. Warenne had then built the enormous castle in the old fort's place, and from his new seat of power, he had granted vast tithes of land, including the port of Hamme, to his loyal baron and good friend Geoffery de Saye – William's great-grandfather.

The church of St Peter and the secrets held there were already tied to the Frankish Templar order, so it was no accident that the port, the church and the promontory were granted to the Saye family by Warenne. Geoffrey de Saye had then granted the Templars land in Saddlescombe, and other powerful barons had provided the Order with further properties and landholdings all over Sussex, securing a very strong base for them on the southern shores of Britain.

William had been a member of the Templar Order for decades now, and had become one of only thirteen men on Earth who knew what was hidden beneath Hamsey Church. His own grandfather had changed the name of Hamme to Hamsey when he had taken ownership of it, adding their own last name to the land, which had now stuck fast. William cursed his aching limbs once more, and let out a fatigued sigh. He had become exhausted by his duties in recent years and had grown tired of the demands put upon the body and mind of a Templar Knight, but his son was still a boy and was not yet ready to assume his responsibilities. His knee crunched alarmingly again, and he grimaced as he made his way up the steep rise to the great hall, perched high above the town. He was getting old, he knew, and longed to take more rest than his duties now afforded him, but that possibility seemed like a distant dream. He approached the doors to the great hall and brought his mind back to the present situation. The guards posted outside the door knew who the Templar Knight was; they were in awe of him, and let him pass without challenge. William had the full trust of the king.

He entered the hall and the king turned to greet him, then stumbled over his overly flamboyant robes, reddened at his clumsiness, and called William forward to discuss the coming battle.

Simon de Montfort's battle lines were formed high on Offham Hill, ready for the assault on Lewes Castle. They looked down the slope to the king's army, gathered in mighty units surrounding the fortification. Simon had been staring at the enemy for many hours now, and it appeared they were in for a tough fight. The numbers were not in their favour, and it seemed the king had also conscripted the help of Templar Knights to his cause. There were not many of the fierce knights, but they had clearly taken control of the army, and would make the assault far more of a challenge than he had hoped for. The Templars would not deter him however; Simon was only one victory away from stripping all power away from the king and securing total control of the country. He could not now turn his army away when he was so close to taking full control, but the only real advantage he had was in holding the high ground, and he planned to use that advantage as best as he could. He knew the king's mind well, and would make use of his impatience this day. He would wait for Henry to attack. He would wait for Henry's troops to charge up the steep slope, and then he would rain lethal clouds of arrows down upon them, slaughtering as many of his soldiers as he could before they reached his lines. It was a good plan, but with one undeniable drawback – the king's Knight seemed well aware of the danger, and neither army had moved forward for most of the day. They were held at an impasse, but it could not last forever.

William stood on the rear slope of the castle's defences, with a good view of the king's army gathered directly below him. On the far hill of Offham, he could just pick out the figure of Montfort and his men, lined up and ready to attack, but it had been more than a day now and still they had not moved. True to form, the king was hiding in his chambers and had left William in charge of his forces and the defence of his throne. It was a wise choice; William was a veteran in the Templar Order and a capable commander. He had seen the danger immediately. To attack Montfort on the steeply rising slope would lead to catastrophic losses to his fighting force and so he had held them back for most of the day, waiting for the usurper to attack first. He had fought in many pitched battles over his years with the Templars, and knew well the folly of charging up steep slopes to engage the enemy, even with superior numbers. If Montfort wanted to win this war, he would have to make the first move; William held the advantage and had simply planned to wait Montfort out, but the king was furious at the delay and had repeatedly sent messengers to William telling him to advance and to kill the traitor. The king was a fool who understood nothing of warfare, thought William once again, but the deadlock would have to be broken soon. There was only so long two armies could stand in battle lines waiting for the other to advance. The tension was becoming unbearable.

Another messenger arrived at William's side. He snatched the note handed to him with the utter disgust he felt whenever he received word from the king. It read simply: 'Attack now, or I will strip you of your title and your lands!' William shook his head, folded the parchment, and sighed in exhaustion at the king's total lack of foresight and courage. The idiot would get them all killed, but sadly, he knew that Henry did not care. The King had lived such a life of privilege that he no longer saw his soldiers as human beings. They were just sheep for him to use as he saw fit. He did not care a whit how many of his men would die, he only cared that Simon de Montfort was brought before him, defeated and ashamed. It could wait no longer, it seemed. William would have to take the fight to the enemy. He had the numbers, along with a unit of highly skilled heavy horsemen, and he would use those advantages to the best of his ability, but it was folly to attack, and he knew it would not end well.

Montfort saw the mounted Templar Knight he suspected was leading the king's army bark out some commands, and messengers quickly moved along their lines. It seemed the battle was about to begin and, as Simon had hoped, the king's man was about to make the first move. It would appear Henry had grown impatient, as Montfort knew he would. He watched intently as the war drums sounded, and the heavy horse, led by the King's son, Edward, began to move towards the foot of the hill below him.

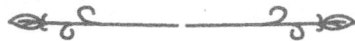

Prince Edward was seething with anger, ready to fight, and tired of waiting for the battle to begin. The upstart baron, Montfort, was attempting to steal away his rightful inheritance, and he would rather die this day than let that come to pass. He had just received the order to attack from William, and he welcomed it. His standard-bearer waved his flag, the war drums sounded, and the heavily armoured horse guard of three hundred men began slowly advancing towards the foot of the slope, organising themselves into a wedge formation before they made their charge. Edward led the men from the front. He ordered his men to raise their shields and lances, and to make ready for the assault, then with a mighty cry to God and Saint George, they kicked their heels hard to their horses' flanks, and began to gather speed as they surged forward as one. The knights hit the bottom of the slope at a fast gallop, then thundered up the hill as fast as their horses were able to carry them.

The terrible carnage began as Montfort's longbowmen released their first volley of armour-piercing bodkin arrows. The man to Edward's right disappeared in an instant as his horse collapsed beneath him. Steel-tipped death rained down upon them and time slowed as the killing began. Edward heard arrows whistling past his head and his horse. His shield arm took the full force of two iron shafts, which penetrated deeply through the top of the wooden rim, but he surged forward and, behind him, his knights were still following in step. He glanced up. At their current distance, Montfort would have time for only one more volley before they hit his lines with their lances. He dipped his head behind his shield once more, and screamed a cry to rally his men. The second wave of death flew at them, from closer range this time, and Edward felt the increased power of the shafts as another bodkin point penetrated his shield, barely missing his arm where he held it through the leather straps. More of his knights fell dead behind him, but others filled the gaps as they appeared. With a mighty crash, they hit the enemy lines with the majority of their force intact, and with savage effect. Edward's lance exploded into fragments as it pierced straight through the torso of his first victim and into a raised shield behind him. That man also went down with the sheer force of the blow, and then Edward dropped the broken shaft and was past him, battering his way deep into the enemy lines as he drew his sword and hacked down at the traitors with vicious efficiency.

At the rear of the king's army, William's shoulders slumped and he looked forlornly on as Edward's heavy horse smashed into Montfort's lines and his foot soldiers charged up the bottom of the slope far behind them. Those heavy horsemen were the best advantage William had been given to occupy the enemy's immediate attention and to give his foot soldiers the valuable time they needed to get up the slope unhindered; but it was not to be. William had screamed in dismay as he watched Edward veer away from the centre of the opposing force. Unwittingly, it seemed, Edward had slid off to the right as he led his charging knights up the steep slope and had succeeded in engaging only the outer edge of Montfort's army. His horsemen were quickly dispatching the enemy there, but they had not achieved the result that William was looking for. Had Edward hit the centre of the lines, William's foot soldiers would have had a fighting chance of following them up the slope and engaging the usurper's soldiers while they struggled to defend themselves against the charging horsemen. But Edward had fouled his task and engaged only one third of the enemy. This would now cost him many soldiers' lives as they made their way up the steep slope towards the centre of Montfort's forces, who were wholly unengaged, and waiting eagerly for them.

The sky darkened once again, and William watched in horror as another cloud of lethal shafts appeared above his army, raining steel-tipped murder down upon his men. The king's struggling soldiers paused for a moment as they attempted to deflect the incoming arrows, then made ready to trudge on again when the projectiles had ceased thumping into their shields, but with such thick volleys coming at them, many shafts were passing through the gaps in their shield walls and taking men down as they crowded together for cover.

On top of the hill, Montfort brought up more archers to the front of his lines, and the new bowmen began loosing their arrows straight down the slope, picking off the king's struggling foot soldiers as they made their way up the hill, their shields raised high to protect them from the arrows raining down on them from above. The thousands of additional arrows Simon had purchased from the village of Fletching were now proving to be worth every ounce of the gold he had paid for them. He narrowed his eyes and bided his time. It was carnage down below, and the majority of his army had barely broken a sweat. His left flank had been initially overwhelmed by the charging horsemen, yet it seemed they were still heavily engaged by his troops there, and currently seemed to pose him little threat.

When his arrows were mostly depleted, and a great many men lay dead on the hill, Montfort charged down the slope and the two forces collided. William's remaining men were now utterly exhausted, while Montfort's men were fresh and ready for battle. Simon hit the king's men three-quarters of the way up the steep slope, and his horsemen cut a deep swathe into the centre of William's fighting force. His foot soldiers followed swiftly after and now horribly outnumbered and outmatched, the real butchery of the king's men began.

William closed his eyes and sighed deeply at the king's stupidity and his son's careless charge. He already knew he had lost this battle, and it would not reflect well on him or his Order, but he was still a Templar Knight and he would not abandon his men on the field. He called his remaining forces together and surged into battle to support his struggling troops as best as he was able, but it was a truly hopeless cause. Before the day was out, the king's army had been pushed back to the Priory by the coastline and William de Saye lay dead amongst the many men on Offham Hill; his sightless eyes staring skyward as the crows descended. The injured screamed in agony, and the dead soaked their blood silently, deep into the earth. Simon de Montfort had won the day.

Epilogue...

King Henry III and his son Edward were both captured by Simon de Montfort on that fateful day in Lewes. Edward was held hostage, but out of pity, Montfort did not execute the king. Instead, he forced him to sign a document named the Mise of Lewes, which ceded nearly all powers of jurisdiction to Montfort. He kept Edward and the king as his prisoners to ensure that Henry abided by the new agreement.

Simon's victory was short lived. Within a year, Edward escaped his confinement and gathered a mighty army together at Evesham to face Montfort in battle once more. Edward won the battle quickly. Simon de Montfort was captured, executed, and dismembered. His body parts were sent to the far corners of the country.

Peter de Molendinis
Year 1307

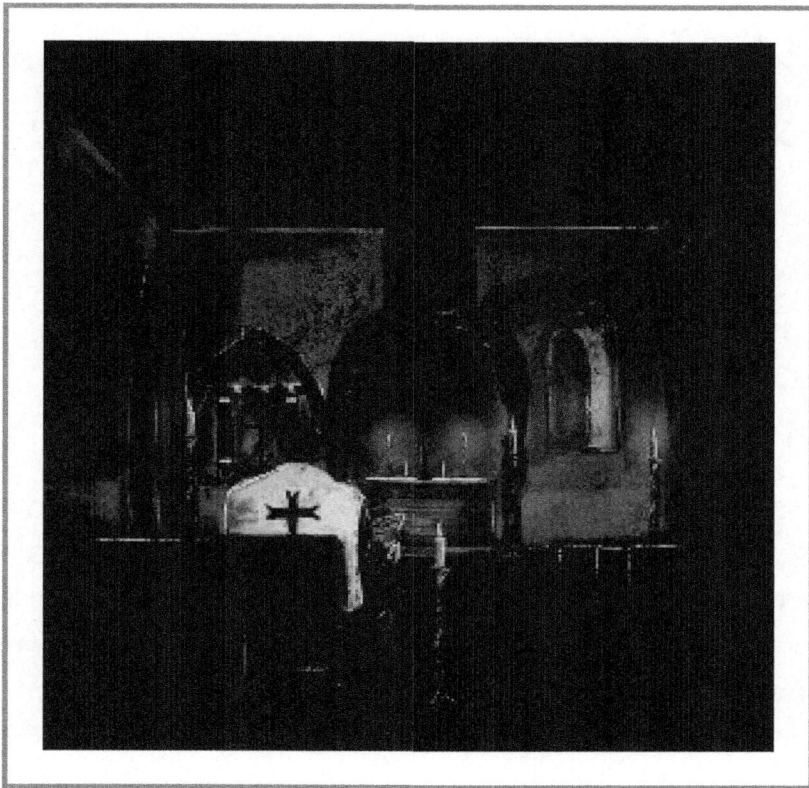

Chapter - 13

Peter de Molendinis
Year 1307

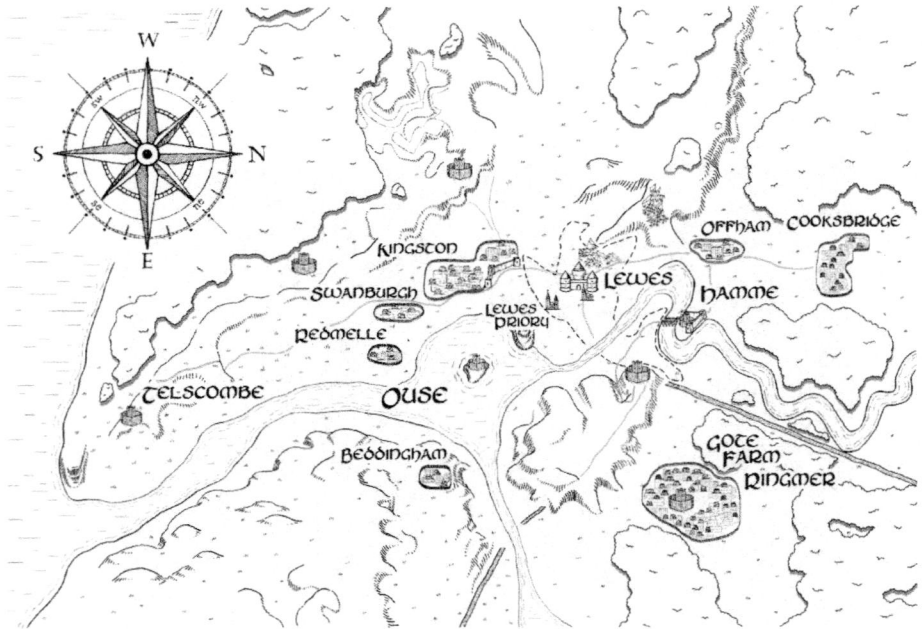

Peter paced restlessly inside St Peter's Church at Hamsey, greatly worried about the news he had just received. His brother Templars were being arrested in droves across the Channel and he knew not why this was occurring. He sat down on a pew to still his nerves and pored over the words once again. The letter read that there were rumours of misdeeds and devil-worship within the Frankish Templar Order, but Peter knew those men and refused to believe that this could be true. They were men of God, hard men but good men; King Philip of France was neither of those things. Peter snarled in irritation at the man's self-proclaimed title of Philip the Fair. From the one encounter that he had suffered with the man, Peter had deduced that Philip was anything but fair, and this trend of lying about oneself to instil a false image in the mind of man was beginning to fill him with disgust. Far worse than that, he had noticed that it was actually working. It seemed that the masses would willingly believe whatever they were told, and the powers across the world were now making great use of this to control the populace and to create false legacies. Peter, however, knew that a house built on a foundation of lies would never stand tall for long. When those lies were exposed, the buildings would come crashing down and their legacy would be as nought. Worse than nought, for they would come to be utterly despised for their deceptions and they would certainly be held accountable for them, whether they knew it or not. Real respect, honour and grace must be earned through truthful deeds; it could not be invented, he mused to himself.

He looked again at the parchment in disbelief. It appeared that some of the more fortunate Templars had been forewarned of Philip's treachery and were now on their way to Hamsey, but others had already been arrested and imprisoned, including the Grand Master, Jacques de Molay. According to the encrypted message, what would soon be arriving at the port was too important to risk falling into the wrong hands; the Templars were bringing with them the entirety of the wealth the organisation had gathered together in France. It did not give specifics, but Peter knew the moment he read between the lines that the Ark would soon be under his care. He worried greatly, but conceded that there really could be no better place to hide it. He had not found himself here by accident; he knew what was beneath his feet. Those secrets had been kept for over a thousand years, passed down through the generations of great men who had built upon the legacy left behind by Joseph and Jeshua here.

Peter's great-grandfather, Rogerius de Molendinis, had held that secret before him. Rogerius had fought alongside Hugues de Payens in the Holy Land and had become the Grand Master of the Hospitaller Knights. When Peter was a young man, his father had shared the secret knowledge of the beginnings of Christianity with him and had brought him to the lands of William de Saye to initiate him into the Order of the Hospitallers. On his death, it had fallen on Peter to become the next guardian of the Grail.

Sitting on the hard wooden bench, he stared through the dirt floor inside the church. Safely stored below him was the body of Christ himself, the Spear of Destiny and the Holy Grail. Peter had seen them all with his own eyes and it had left him in tears. Incredibly, it seemed the Ark too would now be housed in that sacred space beneath the mound. He shook his head in disbelief at what was occurring. It had been difficult to keep these secrets. Difficult, because it meant that reality for Peter was very different from the reality held by other men. This was simply because he knew the truth of the past and they did not. He saw through the veil of lies spinning into existence and they did not. Peter sometimes wondered how he had arrived at this unusual state of existence and if perhaps he was living inside a strange story, written for him alone. So many unbelievable happenings had manifested in his life that it had become difficult not to question the nature of reality; but those complicated musings would have to wait for another time, he thought to himself. He stood and walked to the open door of the church, peering into the night, searching for a sign of the Templar ships making their way over to him from France. The holiest relic of all, the Ark of the Covenant, was on its way to Britain.

He heard the ships before he saw them. The night was pitch-black and the Templars had drawn in their sails long before reaching the coast. They did not want to draw any undue attention to themselves while attempting to hide the entire wealth of the Templar Order, so they had approached quietly, in the depths of the night. The sails had been stowed and the knights were wearing plain black insignia. It would not be wise to allow any folk to identify their colours in that land. They knew that if they were seen this night, someone might speak of their presence here, and it could lead the enemy straight to their door.

The oars dipped and pulled in unison, then were raised and stowed as the two ships coasted into the forward dock on the high tide. Their masts were far too tall to fit under the bridge where a more discreet landing in smaller boats could have been made, but they had far to travel still, and heavy cargo to transport, so mighty Templar ships had been required to undertake the task. Peter strode down to meet them on the wooden wharf as they tied off.

'Brother Peter!' whispered William de Saye as he disembarked, embracing him fiercely.

'Brother William, it is good to see you,' Peter replied, perceiving the worn expression of a tired and hunted man on William's face.

'And you as well, Peter. Would that our meeting had come in better times. Philip has gone mad and arrested the Templar leaders. They struck them at dawn this Friday last – they did not even have a chance to defend themselves!' He shook his head, forlornly. 'I fear the brotherhood as we know it is doomed.'

Peter dipped his head in grim acknowledgement. 'Indeed it does, William. I received word just yesterday eve and have been anticipating your arrival ever since. Philip is a dishonourable man, but I did not think him to be so low as to turn thief in the night, but I am mighty relieved to see you well; and the cargo, William, is it safe?'

William turned his attention back to the boats and smiled broadly. 'That it is, Peter, by the grace of God it is! We must set to work. There is much to move from the boats to the tomb. We must be done and have the ships away before dawn. If we follow our plan to the letter, we may yet preserve what is left of our Order and keep our wealth from King Phillip.'

'And what is the plan, William?' asked Peter. 'You certainly cannot be seen here. The king has many spies in these lands.' He looked around fearfully in the pitch-black of the night, wondering if there were any of the King's informants out there, observing them as they spoke; but all was quiet and the disembarking Knights were quickly scouting the route ahead.

'Fear not, brother, all is in hand. Brother Knights who are not known in these lands will remain with you and don the insignia of the Hospitallers to aid you in our work here for as long as is required. The rest of us will row the boats back out to sea and reconvene with the rest of the fleet. The full fleet will then skirt the coast, out of sight of the mainland. Once past Wales, they will head nearer to the coast once more and reveal their colours as they sail on to Scotland. They will find refuge with the Rosicrucians we have stationed there. Should all go well, none will ever know of our fleeting presence on these southern shores. Rumour will then spread of our final destination and the king's focus will shift to the lands in the north.'

Peter nodded his head and smiled. It was a brilliant plan. If the Templars then staged a defence of the lands in Scotland, it would cement the deception to any who might attempt to recover their wealth in the future. Peter was sure that King Philip would not give up on the treasure so easily, and the Templars' cunning would lead him on a merry chase to nothing. But right now, the ships needed unloading. The secret space beneath St Peter's must remain just that, and so far, no one had even come close to discovering it beneath the innocuous-looking old church. They set to work.

The incredible amount of wealth the Templars had amassed was obscene. Chest after chest of gold and silver, jewels and treasure came up from below decks and were delivered underground into the old Roman bathhouse to sit amongst the ancient treasures of the past already housed there. The sheer volume of wealth filling up the vaults was utterly astonishing.

After countless trips from the boats to the tomb, and when the last of the gold had been safely stored away, the delicate job of moving the Ark then had to be undertaken. In France, the Templars had loaded the Ark on to an enormous cart fitted with a sturdy iron axle. They had then driven it for many hard miles before rolling it on to their great ship, harboured safely at the coast. It was incredibly heavy – the three horses they had tethered to it on this side of the Channel were struggling hard to pull it up the ramp the Knights had created from the ship to the shore, but with much urging in assertive, hushed tones, it finally rose from the boat, and the Ark of the Covenant landed safely on the shores of Britain. It had a large and heavy hessian cloth covering it, pinned down to the cart's edges, securing it in place. Peter stared at its silhouette in awe, longing to see what was beneath that cloth, but also filled with fear and trepidation. He knew the stories that surrounded the Ark. He also knew what incredible power that relic was fabled to contain and that to touch it could mean death.

Steadily and silently, they made their way up the road to the small stone church on the promontory and shortly found themselves through the gates of the old Roman wall, safe from prying eyes, in Templar-held territory. As they slowly rolled the cart towards the church, William assured Peter that much of the myth surrounding the Ark may once have been true, but the relic did not seem to function as it once had; it was no longer dangerous to touch. However, he informed him that it should not be opened under any circumstances. It still contained enough power inside it to send an unprepared man insane.

Once outside the church, the hessian sackcloth was unpinned and Peter's wide eyes beheld the Ark in all its glory, for the first time. It was truly magnificent, and he noted that it was precisely as the passages described it in the Bible: a large wooden chest covered in thick gold, with a solid gold lid. Atop the lid, two astonishing golden cherubim with extended wings faced each other across the mercy seat, and either side of the Ark were large golden hoops, set there to allow long wooden rods to be inserted. It could then be moved without the need for touching such a powerful, holy relic.

The Ark had been found by the Templars in Jerusalem nearly two centuries past. After many hard years of digging beneath Solomon's Mount, the nine original Knights had finally discovered its hiding place. Those great and fearless men had sourced ancient information in the Vatican archives to support the idea that it would be found there. They had then secured and mined that ground relentlessly until they had located it. It had taken many years of backbreaking, secret excavations, but finally, they had found the chamber where Solomon had hidden the Ark. It had been safely stored beneath an ancient structure called the Well of Souls. The only entrance to it had been concreted over, and it appeared that a large stone roof had been purposefully collapsed on top of it to further conceal the area.

It had been hidden there long ago - in times of war, so it would not fall into the enemy's hands. It had then been lost to the world for centuries. In the Order's texts, Peter had read that the Ark had originally come from inside the Great Pyramid in Egypt, where it had functioned in a manner that none could now understand. From there, it had been taken into the world and used as a lethal weapon by Solomon. Solomon had taken it to Jerusalem, the Templars had taken it to France, and now it had found its way over to the shores of Britain. Despite it now being right in front of Peter's eyes, a part of him still struggled to believe it to be true, but there it was, he could not now deny it. The thick wooden rods were inserted into the golden eye-rings, and together the Templars lifted it from the cart. It was incredibly heavy, but with many strong men to call upon, they carried it inside the church, and set it down gently against the back wall. Covering it with the hessian sackcloth once again, they hurried back outside, locking the church door behind them. The cart now had to be removed, and they could not set it on fire for fear of drawing unwanted attention to themselves, so they pulled it over to the lip of the mound, then pushed it over the edge into the boggy land below. Together, they then dragged it out into the estuary and sank it in the deepest part of the river channel they could move it to. The Templar ships had now departed and there was no remaining sign of their landing here. William and his men told Peter that they would now change clothing, depart in a small boat and return in daylight for all the townsfolk to witness, but this time, they would be dressed in the Hospitaller colours. On arrival, they would say to any who asked that they were here to help Peter construct a new chapel area to the church, and that was indeed true, as there was currently no entryway large enough for them to get the Ark into the vault. The Templar Knights would now become Hospitallers, but they would still need to put their legendary masonry skills to good use.

Over the following months, the Templar Knights began their work on the church. They extended the length of the chancel and created a larger opening to get the Ark moved into the vault below. Once they had placed it safely inside, three large flagstones were set into the floor that were left entirely blank. They did not fit well with the existing floor plan, but time was of the essence and stone slabs that were large enough to cover the new entrance could not be purchased without drawing undue attention to the project, so older flagstones were repurposed for the undertaking.

Two decades then passed by before an ill-fated Knight of the Hospitaller Order became slowly poisoned by the treasures they held in those vaults. He had been named as a keeper of the Ark many years ago and since he had first seen it, he had become secretly obsessed with knowing its contents. The thought of it haunted him day and night. He could get no rest and feeling driven to madness, he decided that he simply had to see what was contained within it.

He bided his time, and soon succeeded in recruiting another Knight to his cause. Together, in the depths of night, they quietly removed the flagstone, and entered the vault. With great care and much trepidation, they strained their muscles hard against the weight of gold, and removed the lid to the Ark. It was incredibly heavy and was so well fitted, it seemed a vacuum had formed within it. Air hissed in loudly as the strong seal was broken.

They set the lid aside carefully, and then in awe, they slowly moved their torches closer to the golden chest. The flickering orange light reflected on the contents within.

Two stone tablets filled the vast majority of the space, one sitting on top of the other. They were enormous, and were inscribed with beautiful, ancient writing. The laws of God, set in stone. The inscriptions seemed flawless, and in stunning confirmation of the Bible story, they could see five distinct lines on the uppermost tablet. Though neither was able to translate the text, they both knew what it was purported to say. They grinned at each other, wide-eyed in excitement, and examined the tablet further before turning their attention to the only other item within the Ark. Fitting neatly in the gap between the foot of the large stones and the inside wall of the chest was a small golden box that looked very similar to the Ark itself, only longer and slimmer. They lifted it out, and set it down on the floor of the vault to view its contents.

A small amount of fine white powder puffed into the air as they released the sturdy catch. The hinged lid swung slowly open and they both took stock of the strange item within. It was a rod of what looked like a metal, about as thick and long as a forearm. It was heavy, and other than its smooth and silvery surface, there seemed to be nothing else remarkable about it. Once they had examined it thoroughly, confused at its purpose, they put everything back as they had found it, then replaced the lid to the Ark. No one would ever know they had been there this night, and they swore an oath to never speak of their actions again, even to each other. The Knight was pleased and well relieved at the success of his dangerous mission and the discoveries he had made, and for the first time in months he slept like a baby, but unbeknownst to him, that was the final period of peace he would ever experience in his life.

He awoke early the next morning and stumbled as soon as he stood from his bed. His balance had deserted him. He tottered toward the wall of his room and reached out a hand to stop the impact. It was then that he felt the searing pain in his fingers. He looked at them through foggy eyes and saw to his horror that the skin was heavily burned and seemed to be peeling away from the bones beneath. The pain was suddenly excruciating. Terror seized his heart, and a guttural scream surged up from within him. He bellowed his fear into the dawn. Fitting violently, he collapsed in a heap on to the stone floor.

His brother Hospitallers found him there, writhing in agony, only a minute later. He seemed to be covered in sores and burns, his peeling flesh leaving him horrifyingly disfigured.

None could fathom what had happened to him, so they did what they could to make him comfortable, but the Knights had few medicines available to them and they were unable to alleviate his pain in the least. The poor soul had mostly screamed himself to death before his heart gave up on him and blissful silence filled his quarters once more. It was brief. Mere minutes passed by before the second victim was discovered, also howling in unnatural agony, and then the third came, and the fourth…

A nightmare of torment ensued, and as the sun set on that horrific day, the Knights stationed there had barricaded themselves inside the fortification. It seemed that no outsiders were yet afflicted by this devastating illness and, with their isolated position, boats could be warned away as they approached. Quarantine seemed like the best option to stop the mysterious disease from spreading, so they walled themselves in.

Word was sent to the Hospitallers in nearby lands, but by the time they arrived just days later, they discovered only three surviving Knights, who had fled the area at the outset on the prudent advice of their brothers. All the other men inside the enclosure were now dead, and not even the crows seemed willing to go near the corpses.

<hr />

The Hospitallers kept that place locked away from the world and well guarded for the better part of a year before they allowed one man to enter, who had bravely volunteered to scout the ground and see if the disease was still present. He spent many hours looking around that miserable place for any clues to the cause of the tragedy. The pain in the atmosphere that surrounded him was palpable. The bodies he found were mostly decomposed and unrecognisable, but the screams of twisted agony could still be seen on many of their desiccated faces. There seemed to be no apparent cause to explain the event, and after he had spent three days inside the walled-off promontory with no sign of illness, others slowly dared to join him. Tentatively, and with great care not to touch the bodies with their bare hands, they burned the dead in a mighty pyre and scrubbed the whole complex clean. A dozen cats were brought in to keep the rats and vermin under control and after many months, it seemed that the disease would not return, but the memory of that terrible time could still be felt there, even centuries later.

<hr />

Epilogue…

As the years passed by, Britain fell into the cold grip of a mini ice age. The temperatures plummeted low enough that the river Thames in London froze solid. The ice became so thick that markets and bonfires were often held on it. The locals called them Frost Fairs.

On the southern shores, as the ocean began to form into ice caps once more, the sea levels began to recede, leaving many once important locations, now unreachable by larger boats. Pevensey Castle was left stranded seven miles from the new coastline, and the Ouse became a narrow river that frequently silted up from the steep terrain that surrounded it. Lewes and Hamsey were no longer suitable as port towns. Slowly, they began to lose their important place in the world. The features and forts that had once made that incredible valley so very desirable, were no longer of any great use, and they quickly fell into ruin.

The remarkable history that had been birthed on those shores was soon forgotten by most; but the descendants of the Templars, the Hospitallers and the Masons, kept close to their hearts those great secrets, that soon only the highest in their orders would become privy to.

Richard Woodmancote
Year 1557

Chapter - 14

Richard Woodmancote
Year 1557

…Wherefore, dear brethren and sisters to whom this my writing shall come, be of good cheer, and fear not what man can do unto you; for they can but kill the body, but fear him that hath power to kill both body and soul. And yet once again I bid you be of good cheer; for the sheriff, with diverse other gentlemen and priests, whilst I was at the sheriff's house, said to me that all the heretics in the country hung on me, as the people did in times past upon St. Augustine or St. Ambrose or suchlike. Wherefore said they, 'Look well on it; you have a great thing to answer for.'

Richard set down his quill; the temperature had dropped alarmingly since the sun had set and he could not stop shivering. The stone blocks of his dismal jail cell oozed with dirty water as the rain lashed down hard on the street above. A small window with thick iron bars looked out on to the pavement from a narrow opening at the top of the wall. Of humanity, he had seen only feet for three days now, and it had begun to feel like they were mocking his captivity as they passed him by. A drop of water fell on his head again, forcing out a grimace as it rolled down his neck. Richard shifted his position on the wooden bench, rubbed his crossed arms fiercely to stay warm, and returned to his only other form of entertainment; contemplating the Bible while staring at the patterns on his cell wall.

He had to face it. It had been a foolish decision to let himself be led here by the Bishop's men. They had provided him with no warrant, therefore he had not been legally obliged to go with them. He knew this, yet he had gone with them anyway. In his naivety, somewhere in his confusion, he had hoped that he might receive some sensible answers to many genuine concerns he had regarding his interpretations of the Bible. Richard's logical mind was unwilling to accept that such simple questions could have caused so much of a stir. But he should have known that he would not be heard by the Bishop. He should have known his questions would remain unanswered, twisted and derided. He should have bloody known. His faith in God and his utter dedication to truth had brought him to this miserable place, but despite the awful conditions he now found himself in, he had at last resigned himself to the situation. He would willingly pay the price for his actions, for he would not live a lie, no matter how insistent others were in imposing their beliefs on him. Very soon he would become a martyr, and there was nothing he could do to stop it.

It had all begun with the arrival of a profoundly powerful book. The very moment the translated English Bible had appeared on the shores of Britain, the Catholic Church had made it illegal to possess. It was forbidden knowledge to any but their elected clergy, but many people were greatly interested in what the mysterious tome spoke of. They had listened to strange, foreign words being recited to them while attending church services their whole lives, and only a minority of learned individuals had been able to understand what the priests were actually saying. This unknown, ancient language had once lent an air of ceremonial magic to the proceedings, but since the English translation had arrived in the country it was slowly losing its ability to enthral the masses. Those endless Latin mumblings had created an illusion of mysterious incantation that only the priests had access to, and now, despite the English Bible being illegal to own, many people were deeply curious about its contents, and were willing to take the risk of owning a copy to discover its secrets.

Richard became consumed with it. He had read the book quickly, in its entirety, and his views on the events described within seemed astonishingly at odds with what he had been led to believe his whole life. He had been gifted with an incredibly sharp mind and had memorised the entire text, chapter and verse, by his third reading of it. With it now stored away safely in his mind, he was capable of instantly recalling any passage he wished to revisit. This had allowed him to study the deeper meanings behind the words at his leisure, and over the many years he had been contemplating the remarkable stories it contained, he had come to some very different conclusions than those that had been taught to him by the Catholic Church.

One of the most conflicting problems he could not reconcile his new knowledge with was the Catholic sacramental service. As far as Richard could tell, the wine and the wafer were clearly described as being symbolic of Christ's blood and flesh. They did not actually transform into those things during the ritual as he had been led to believe. There seemed to be no information in the entire text that supported the Catholics' assertion on this matter, and yet they only seemed able to defend their position with intimidation and outrage; they had no reasonable answers for him at all.

The second, and most contentious, problem he had was that the beliefs of all the churches in the land seemed to be changing dramatically, depending largely on which monarch was in power. To wholeheartedly give yourself to one set of beliefs, only for them to them to be completely changed across the country just days after the death of a king was too much for Richard to accept. He had said as much to his local priest, and this had been the beginning of the end for him. The cleric had reddened with rage at Richard's assertion that he was quite clearly a hypocrite, and had immediately sent for the sheriff to arrest him for blasphemy.

Richard had spent many months living like a wild man in the woods after that day, giving the villainous clerks who had come to arrest him a merry runaround, which he had enjoyed immensely. But finally, the day came when they had caught him, and sadly, it had not been because of their skill and cunning that they had found him, but because his brother-in-law had betrayed him, revealing his secret hiding place to the sheriff.

Richard had squeezed himself into a narrow, panelled wall above a window in his home. On many previous occasions, the officers had searched his rooms while he had lain hidden there and they had not even come close to finding him. But not this time. When the clerks began to poke at the wooden panel he was hidden behind the moment they entered his home, he knew he had been betrayed. Richard had then broken out through the thatched roof to escape, but had instantly seen there was nowhere to run; they had him surrounded, and to their great satisfaction, he was captured by the Bishop's men.

Richard requested he see the warrant for his arrest, which they had not provided him with. They told him that they had forgotten to bring it, but assured him that it did exist, and would be found back at one of the men's lodgings in the village. They told him that they could retrieve it for him when they all arrived there, but he did not believe their words and had refused to accompany them. It was not lawful for them to arrest him without it, he informed them. The sheriff had then reasoned with Richard, promising on his honour that if he accompanied him to the lodgings of the Bishop of Chichester to answer the charges brought against him, he would not be treated unfairly. Richard was extremely tired of being a hunted man, and his certainty that he was correct in his assertions and that he could prove his arguments clearly, had led him to wearily capitulate. After gathering his jacket and boots, he had let himself be led away. But it was now clear as glass that he had made a bad decision, for his words had immediately offended the Bishop and riled him up in to a rage, and now he found himself here, freezing to death in a damp jail cell; but he would not be cold tomorrow, for tomorrow he would burn.

Richard shook his head again in angry confusion. How vile and deceitful people had become over these last months. It seemed utterly astonishing to him that everyone else in the country was just going along with this obvious and dramatic change to their freedoms and their faith without voicing any concern at all. At first, he thought they were all just pretending for the sake of a simple life, but he now realised that this was not the case. He had not understood how weak, scared and easily deceived the masses were; how willingly they would alter everything they believed in for fear of reprisals from assumed authority. Many folk had even begun informing on their own families, just to be heralded for being on the right side of the ever-changing laws. Approval from their government and popular, accepted opinion had proven to be more important to them than any other virtue; even more important than their own friends and family. It was hard to acknowledge just how many grown adults were still just frightened children, begging for their elders' approval. He had found himself to be living in a nest of spineless snakes, and it sickened Richard to his very core. He had thought better of humanity, and was glad to be leaving them behind. He would indeed suffer tomorrow, he knew, but only for a few agonising minutes; they, however, would have to suffer each other for eternity.

Epilogue…

Along with nine other heretics, Richard was led through a busy street full of sombre-looking souls the next morning. Many had gathered to watch the horrifying, yet strangely compelling spectacle. There, the ten prisoners were tied to a stake outside of the Star Inn in Lewes, the pyre was lit, and the men and women - screamed in agony as they burned. The crowd watched, mesmerised.

Those ten poor souls were cruelly put to death for their refusal to accept old ideals they thought humanity had long since transcended. They were burned for disagreeing with the words of another. They were burned for speaking their own truth. But to their great credit, they remained steadfast in their own faiths, and they died free.

During the five years of her reign, Mary Tudor committed nearly three hundred innocent souls to the fire in terrible retribution for Henry VIII's dismissal of the Catholic Church. This was quite unremarkable for Mary; her father had ordered the execution of tens of thousands while he had reigned. They were only common people; easily cowed into obedience with misinformation, gross displays of violence and threats of terrible punishment.

In the year 1557, at the time of Richard's execution – the people had seen these victims as heretics. However, in 1563 a new book was published in Britain; it was called 'Foxes book of Martyrs'. The enormous work was three times as long as the bible and captured in vivid detail, the history of the martyred protestants at the hands of the Roman Catholic church. The publicist, John Fox, included sixty, grisly illustrations, vividly capturing the "persecutions and horrible troubles, wrought and practiced by the Roman Prelates."

This was the beginning of the end for Catholicism in Britain. Those gruesome stories and shocking images, slowly embedded themselves in to the consciousness of the populace and soon, Catholic services were banned throughout the country for time immemorial and the one time heretics were now hailed as martyrs.

The use of media to manipulate the perceptions of the public had now begun in earnest. The battle for belief raged on.

Nicholas Poussin
Year 1620

Chapter - 15

Nicholas Poussin
Year 1620

'Welcome, Nicholas. All has been made ready.' The rector clasped his hands together and bowed to his fellow initiate.

"Greetings, Brother Wood,' he replied, bowing in return. Nicholas was nervous; he sensed his world was about to change dramatically in the course of the next few hours. Rector Edward Wood was about to reveal the highest secret of their Order. He was feeling deeply uneasy, but was also genuinely excited to find out what that secret was. More than anything now, he hoped he would not be disappointed. It had taken him a very long time to infiltrate the Order and to work his way up the ranks, and he truly hoped the trouble of doing so would now be worth it.

Edward motioned for Nicholas to follow him, then led him up to the small church on the promontory. They entered through the front porch into the nave, then turned to their right and entered the chancel. The church had the cold and dusty smell of ages about it, yet there was an atmosphere of great reverence inside the building. Many candles were burning, and they flickered gently as the two hooded men in black cassocks closed and locked the door behind them. The clang of the bolt echoed ominously in the sparsely furnished space.

Nicholas turned his gaze to the right and saw a beautiful golden cross standing on a tomb at the end of the chancel. To the side of this was the covered mortuary tomb of the de Saye family, who had held these lands for many centuries. He looked to his feet. Usually set securely within the floor, a large flagstone had been lifted in front of the altar and a simple ladder led down from there to the vaults below. Edward handed Nicholas a lantern and descended into the ancient space beneath the earth. Nicholas followed nervously after him.

Nicholas was still in shock. He had never imagined he would actually see what he had just witnessed below the church and it had left him dumbstruck. He had requested time to process it all, and Edward had left him with the key to the church, to sit and contemplate once his brother masons had replaced the flagstone and re-pointed the joints, leaving no trace of the ground's disturbance.

The Ark was beautiful. He knew he would never forget it; there was an aura of profound mystery and power that surrounded it, and the image of it was now burned into his memory. The Grail cup was also magnificent, and to have been allowed to hold such a holy item was one of the greatest moments of his life. Then there was the spearhead, the actual spearhead that had pierced Christ's side was also down there, kept alongside the Grail, but far more important than all of the treasures he had seen, was Jeshua's actual ossuary box, containing his skull and his bones. Jesus Christ, son of Joseph, was a real man; it was all beyond Nicholas' wildest dreams. To bear witness to such fabulous treasures was more than he could have ever hoped for. He had been looking for those answers his whole life. He had longed to know the truth of the past, and now he had walked among it, his life felt transformed.

He opened his sketchbook, took the piece of charcoal wrapped in tissue from his top pocket, then sat down directly above the vault and began to sketch the tomb located there. It was beautifully crafted. Stonemasons of the highest skill must have chiselled that blockwork.

Nicholas had learned how to pay attention to minute details while mastering his craft, and noticed now some interesting shadows on the blocks he could incorporate into his sketch. However, when he looked again he saw nothing nearby to cast those shadows, so he got up and examined them closer. He realised at last that they were in fact dark stains inherent in the blocks themselves. He thought about that for a while, and smiled as an idea came to him. He could not reveal the secret of this place, for he was a man of his word, and he could not and would not break his oath, but he could leave a subtle clue behind that perhaps somebody might decipher in the future. He would set to work on his preliminary sketches when he returned to his family home in Dieppe.

Epilogue...

Nicholas went on to paint many masterpieces in his lifetime. He packed them with mystery, atmosphere and biblical symbology; all subtly pointing to the greater secrets in life. He finished one of his finest pieces, 'The Shepherds of Arcadia', on his arrival in Rome, sparking the beginnings of a great mystery that would not be solved for four hundred years... Blue Apples.

Thomas Anson
Year 1758

Chapter - 16

Thomas Anson
Year 1758

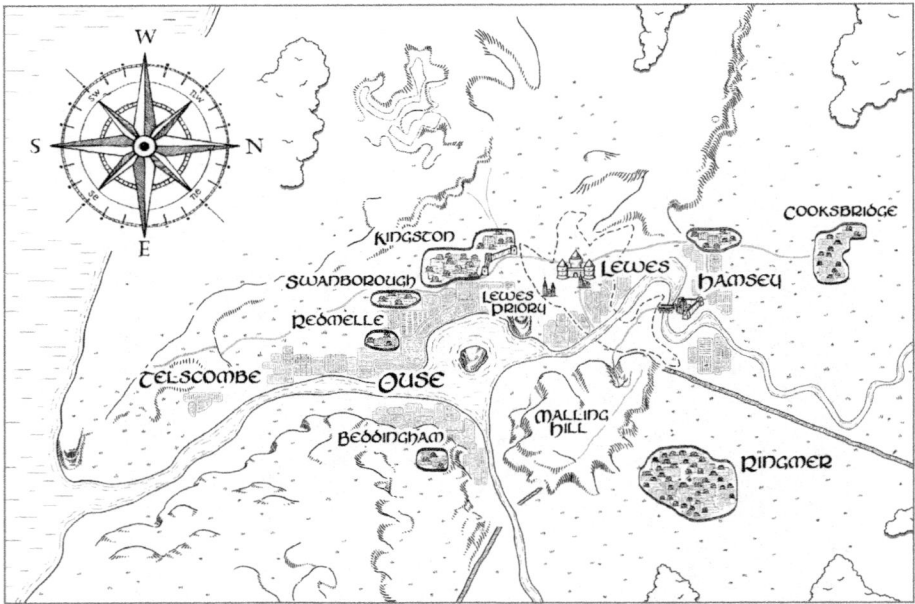

Thomas was in shock once more. He could not quite process what he had just witnessed inside the church of St Mary at the foot of Lewes. The congregation there were in disarray. When the blue lightning ball had shot through the church roof just minutes past, the force of it had thrown the congregation from their pews. They were all stunned and unable to gather their wits. Was God trying to get their attention? Surely he must be, thought Thomas; there could be no clearer sign. Thomas tried to recall the sermon the dean had been reading when it had happened but he had stopped listening to the miserable mumblings long ago, as had most of the congregation. Church had become a punishment for them all. No one wanted to spend their Sunday listening to a man of God droning on for hours, with what seemed to be an utter disinterest for the words he was reciting. The people only went to these services now because they feared the repercussions if they did not. There was nothing joyous or loving about the occasion. Quite the opposite – it seemed that the re-invented church was far more intent on making the congregation feel guilty and fearful. It was a tool they had been using for many years to control and profit from the populace, and it had worked. Smallpox was ravaging the land, and in terror of the hideous death, people had now turned to God, and as far as they had been led to believe, God was only accessible through the church.

The church leaders had become forces to be reckoned with; they had gained enormous wealth and terrifying influence over the last two centuries and they had now begun to utilise the outlawed Catholic ways in order to retain that power. Only three years past, they had continued with the old tradition of burning 'witches and heretics' at the stake outside of the Star Inn. This hideous display of an agonising death had very successfully cowed the local population into compliance once again. The punishment had been used for centuries now, and the threat was very simple; obey, agree, or die in an excruciating manner. The deans, deacons and scribes now walked the streets with delusions of grandeur and an air of haughtiness from their powerful positions that the townsfolk despised. Many decent folk had known the men and women who had been executed that day. They had also known that they were honest, decent people, who were largely innocent of the charges brought against them; at the least, they had certainly not deserved to die in that manner. But they also knew that the church officials were not above spreading vicious lies to assert their assumed authority; they could accuse any one of them of heresy at any moment should they should show even a hint of dissent. Too few had the clarity of vision, wit or courage to band together and stop the madness, so they sheepishly attended services every Sunday, though they all loathed being held in that cold prison. Fear was the most effective tool the church, and the monarchies around the world, had used to control the masses for centuries.

Thomas remembered then that the large donations bowl had been beginning its weekly rounds when the lightning ball had struck. In an awesome show of power, it seemed that God had sent a clear message to the priest and the congregation with a weapon from the heavens. It was a most curious thing. The ball of lightning had struck the roof with an almighty force, then entered through it as a blue orb with an orange tail, curving sharply before it hit the ground, then shooting off through the aisle. The doors to the church had blown open as it approached them, and just metres beyond, it had exploded like a mighty cannon, shattering windows and knocking people from their feet. None were severely injured, which was a miracle in itself considering the damage it had done to the buildings surrounding it. Mr Baldy's shop across from the church had lost its windows but was still standing. Part of the church roof was seriously damaged, and melted lead had been blown into the street. A piece of stone from the tower had also been thrown across the road.

The more fearful folk in the congregation were now praying hard, offering pious apologies for whatever it was they assumed they had done; rocking back and forth in stunned shock. Thomas was not afraid in the least. He had witnessed a great many strange things in his time within the Hospitaller Order. Long ago, he had been initiated as a guardian of the secrets held at Hamsey, and was quite used to odd occurrences manifesting in his life. This, however, was a new experience he had really not expected; his ears were still ringing from the explosion. He wiggled a finger into one and shook his head to clear it, but the ringing persisted. He hoped that, with a bit of luck, it would clear itself up in time. He had only come to this service to keep up appearances during his yearly visit to the church at Hamsey, but as was often the way in his life, he suspected that it was not mere chance that had led him there. He was already having serious misgivings regarding the direction the church was moving in, but the Order was powerful, and he had sworn an oath to the Hospitallers that he could not now break.

Epilogue…

Years passed by for Thomas, and the feeling would not leave him. There was something horribly wrong with how the church and the Order were functioning in the world. It had left a bitter taste in his mouth. He had become a very wealthy man by joining their ranks, but at some level, he felt that perhaps he had sold his soul, and it did not sit well with him. He thought again to the monument he had created at his home in Shugborough, and hoped dearly that someone who had sworn no oaths to anyone would someday figure out the map he had left for them after he died. No one in the Order knew of his monument. In fact, it seemed that no one in the Order but he - had even understood what Poussin had done those many years past.

After Thomas had been initiated into the Thirty-Third Degree at Hamsey, he had spent time alone at the church, slowly coming to terms with what he had witnessed below it. He had seen the original 'Shepherds of Arcadia' painting many years before he had arrived there. It had taken him little time to recognise its twin when he had seen it in the real world. Thomas immediately understood what Poussin had done, and he had to admit that it was a stroke of genius. Simple shadows and a little finger, subtly pointing the way to a mystery he too had longed to share with the world. It was now Thomas' turn to do the same, and he had commissioned his sculpture to be a mirror image of the 'Shepherds of Arcadia' painting. He hoped that, in time, somebody might recognise the sculpture and link it to Poussin's painting. Perhaps they would then study it a little closer. But this would not be enough, he feared. If Thomas had not known what lay beneath his feet that day, he suspected he would never have linked the painting to the tomb, so Thomas decided he would inscribe a code beneath the carving to lead people to the church at Hamsey. He had made it as clear as he was able to without completely giving the game away. The origins of the tomb had begun in the Roman era, so he had used Latin lettering. The D M would stand for Dis Manibus, referring to the Roman Manes, the spirits of the dead. Above and between those two letters he had inscribed OUOSVAVV. These letters represented the following:

'Supported by the spirits of the dead, at the end of the Ouos I came to God's house. I saw, I conquered.'

He made sure that none of his Order would ever see it before he died and commissioned many more sculptures in his gardens, so as not to bring unwanted attention to what would otherwise be the sole monument in his grounds. It was over a century before they realised what he had done.

Thomas Paine
Year 1771

Chapter - 17

Thomas Paine
Year 1771

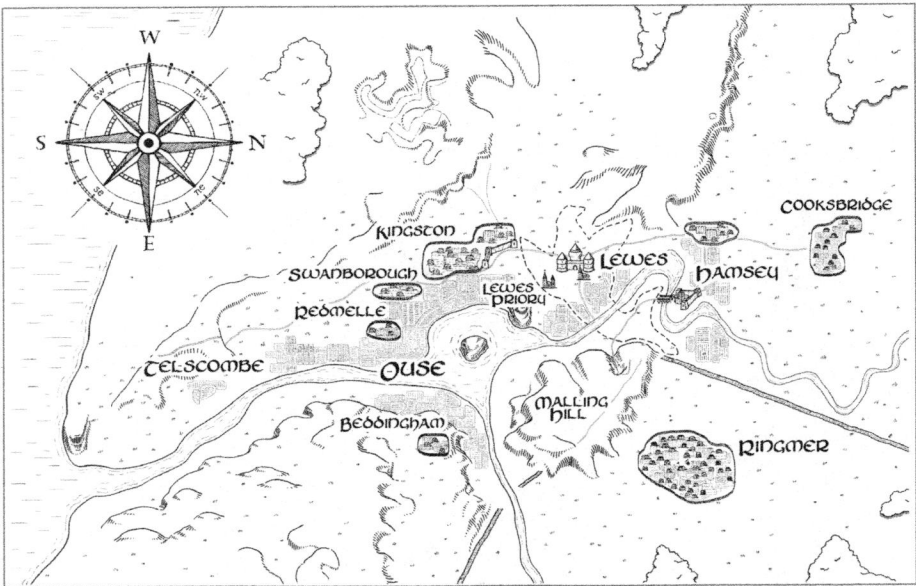

'Sweep yer chimney, sir?' asked the grubby little boy, his face black with soot, framing sunken, hungry eyes.

Thomas looked down at the poor wretch on his doorstep. He had only had his chimney swept a few weeks ago, but it was snowing outside and the little lad looked on the verge of death. The poor boy shivered uncontrollably as he waited for his answer, and Thomas decided to take pity on the child.

'How much?' he asked him.

'Two pennies sir,' he replied.

'Well, you'd better come in, young man.' Thomas waved him inside, relieved to shut out the bitter cold once more as he closed the door behind him.

'Thank you, sir. Freezing out there it is, but I do so love the snow.'

Thomas took stock of the boy. He was a waif of a child, and whilst starvation was not uncommon amongst the overcrowded population, seeing the true state of the lad up close was most disturbing.

'How long is it since you last ate something, boy?' asked Thomas, genuine concern furrowing his brow.

'Only a day, sir, only a day,' the lad replied cheerfully. He had quickly learned not to moan about his life, and just to get the job done; nobody was interested in the complaints of a street boy, and if he put on a smile, they would sometimes ask him to come back. In truth, though, this was the umpteenth house he had now tried to win a job at, and he was on his last reserves of energy.

Thomas motioned to his table and set an old newspaper down on a chair. 'Sit down, and I will fetch you some hot food. My wife has just finished preparing some gruel for our lunch. You may join us, if you wish?'

The boy looked confused. 'This a trick, sir?' he asked suspiciously, narrowing his eyes.

'No trick, young man, but you may sweep the chimney and leave, if you would prefer?'

The child thought about it for a while. Kindness was not a quality he had often experienced in his short life, and he'd heard stories of other lads being tricked and abused. This man looked genuine enough, though, and he supposed that if he lived in a building as grand as Bull House, he would most likely be wealthy enough to really have extra food to spare. Hunger got the better of him, and he took a seat. Thomas left him at the table for a moment, returning shortly afterward with his wife, and three hot bowls of thick gruel.

'There you are, young man.' He motioned toward the lady who had joined him. 'This is my wife, who we have to thank for our meal.' Thomas set the bowls down, and they both took their seats.

'Hello.' The lady introduced herself. 'I am Elizabeth Paine, and what is your name?'

'Name's Jack, Miss Elizabeth.'

She smiled warmly at the filthy little lad. 'Nice to meet you, Jack.' She passed him a spoon. He took it and waited for Thomas and Elizabeth to eat a few mouthfuls, still unsure if he could really trust these people; but his belly growled loudly, and he found he could hold out no longer. He plunged the spoon into the thick gruel, and attacked it with astonishing speed.

They spoke little during their meal, discovering only that Jack was six years old and lived in a poorhouse down by the docks. He was understandably shy and suspicious, so they did not press him to talk any further. Jack had wolfed down his bowl of gruel in seconds and, feeling horribly affected by the boy's plight this day, Thomas offered him his own, which he devoured with similar determination. Once they had finished, Elizabeth cleared away their bowls and Thomas showed the boy the chimney he needed to be swept.

Jack set to work removing the fire grate, then set down his blackened cloth in its place to collect the falling soot. Grabbing his brush, he clambered inside the horribly narrow space and set to work. It did not take him long to get the task done, and once he had finished the filthy job, a significant amount of coke had come down from above. Thomas wondered if the last boy had done any cleaning at all while he was up there. It would seem he had needed his chimney swept after all.

He gave the boy three pennies and told him to hide one away, somewhere only he knew of, and far away from his minder. Thomas knew how the poor-gangs worked. Jack would hand over everything he earned. In return, he would receive a place to sleep and a few scraps of food; it was a truly awful existence. Many of these working children died at an exceptionally young age, but the alternatives were not much better. The poor laws were just not sufficient to serve the growing population any longer, but change was hard to accomplish. It had to begin somewhere, however, thought Thomas, so he would bring the issue up during the society meeting at the White Hart this very evening. The Headstrong Club were gathering for their weekly debate.

It had begun as a small group of learned individuals discussing important matters and formulating strategies for furthering their ideas, but it was growing very quickly. Unfortunately, many new faces had recently joined their party whose company Thomas did not enjoy. He felt like he was being argued with at every opportunity of late, and the newcomers' arguments were flawed, irritating and distracting. They consumed much of the group's time and attention, and Thomas' patience was running out. These men of high standing had suddenly and strangely appeared from out of nowhere. They seemed far more interested in subtly disrupting proceedings with inane arguments than in debating anything of substance. Thomas had decided to end the charade this very night.

Thanking the young boy for his work, Thomas saw him to the door. Jack tipped his felt hat to Thomas and Elizabeth and thanked them for the job and the food. They smiled kindly at him and requested he return in a few weeks to do the job again, to which he happily agreed.

With an unusually full belly for the first time in weeks, money to satisfy his gang-master, and a penny of his own to spend as he liked, Jack sauntered off down the high street feeling like a victorious king.

The fire was burning beautifully that evening as Thomas put on his best black jacket over his waistcoat, straightened out the stiff cuffs, and brushed some lint off his hat before placing it neatly on his head. He examined himself in the mirror. Feeling suitably well dressed and groomed, he bade his wife a good evening, kissed her on the cheek, then picked up his walking cane and braced himself for the cold temperature outside. He would not have to endure it for long, he assured himself – the White Hart was only a minute down the road. He stepped into the high street, shut the door behind him and checked his fob watch. He would be right on time.

The wind rushed by in violent gusts, with freshly falling snow blowing hard into his face as he began his short journey. Thomas quickly grabbed hold of his hat as a howling blast picked up speed momentarily, threatening to dislodge it from his head. Shoving it back down hard, he strode on through the thick snow.

In a well-practised, unconscious action, he glanced up to his left. The spire on St Michael's Church was still there, tilting precariously, high above him. It was so very steep that little snow had gathered on the small, weathered shingles. Thomas had always thought the spire looked much like a rickety old wizard's hat. He often wondered how it was still standing, yet it certainly seemed able to endure all sorts of violent weather he had witnessed since he had arrived here. Nonetheless, he always had to make sure it was still upright when he passed it by.

He glanced forward once again, squinting his eyes and holding a hand in front of his face to lessen the wintry assault somewhat as he trudged on through the snow. Passing the entrance to Lewes Castle on his left, he smiled at the sight of the beautiful old ruins. Thomas was fascinated by history. He knew well of the king's defeat to Simon de Montfort here. Lewes had become a hotbed of anti-royalist and progressive types since that day. A grand, and somewhat pagan, celebration had also begun to take place here over the last century. Contrary to popular belief, in honour of Guy Fawkes, and a devout group of Catholics who had attempted to blow up the Houses of Parliament whilst full of influential Protestant men in 1605, a great bonfire night had quickly become an annual event, which took place here on the fifth of November. Guy Fawkes had failed that day, but the rebellion lived on. The people were well relieved that Catholicism had now been banned in the country but they had also applauded the attempt to destroy the corrupted government. The high street looked very different during that riotous evening, with bonfires, torched processions, drummers and all sorts of wild behaviour that, by the very next morning, was all but forgotten. Despite some early efforts, there seemed little the authorities could do to stop this remarkable, recurring event from going ahead. They did not have the policing manpower to stop it, and the people who lived in this town were no longer the meek peasants of old, but a waking populace, who had begun to truly understand the cavernous divide between rich and poor, and who were fearless enough to express their dissatisfaction openly at the great inequality. Bonfire Night had become a symbol of freedom to the people.

Thomas trudged on, past the warm glow coming from the windows of the Old Star Inn on the other side of the trackway, and was soon outside the White Hart. He pushed open the door, entered quickly, then shut it swiftly behind him. Removing his hat, he brushed it off and cleaned his boots. A butler took his jacket from him, then opened the door to the busy room beyond. Thomas stepped into the warm and welcoming space, quickly making his way to the large fireplace to warm up his hands. His good friend Clio appeared by his side, presenting him with a brandy. Thomas received it gratefully.

'That'll warm you back up, Thomas.'

'Thank you, Clio,' Thomas replied. His eyes scoured the room, quickly falling on the faces he had begun to greatly resent seeing in the group.

'Many of them here tonight?'

'Same as last time, it would seem,' Clio replied. He tapped out the ash from his clay pipe into the fire, then filled the bowl with some fresh tobacco.

Forced, raucous laughter rolled across to them from the group of four men by the bar. Thomas winced. They had an air of privilege about them that he simply despised, and yet it was not their wealth that he loathed, it was their arrogance, greed and deep sense of entitlement. They lived in the same world as he, filled with suffering and poverty, yet they seemed not to care, or even notice, and their casual, snooty attitude irked Thomas enormously. He had never spent much time around men such as these, but it was not an experience he now wished to repeat any more than was strictly necessary.

Clio struck a match and lit his pipe.

'Are we still agreed?' asked Thomas.

Clio nodded his head slowly. He flicked his wrist to extinguish the match in a well-practised motion, and threw it on to the fire.

'We are all agreed, Thomas.'

Thomas held the floor.

'Tonight, I wish to discuss a truly important matter. During the past days, weeks and years, I have become increasingly appalled with the conditions and treatment of children in our society. The population is growing very fast and the slums are vastly overcrowded. Crime and theft are increasing due to starvation. Children are commonly worked to death before being tossed into the street. Boys and girls as young as six are being hanged on the gallows. This is a crime against humanity, and if we do not act to change the poor laws to better care for our people's needs, I fear this state of affairs will become an accepted norm. That is not a world I wish to live in.'

One of the newcomers, Edmund Burke, Thomas thought his name was, broke with club protocol for the umpteenth time that evening and threw his opinion at Thomas from the back of the room.

'God made the rich and the poor, sir. Poverty is an unavoidable part of life, it would seem.' His colleagues nodded their agreement and waited for Thomas to respond.

'I disagree, sir,' Thomas rebutted. 'It is wrong to say that God made rich and poor; he made only male and female, and he gave them the earth for their inheritance.'

Edmund had no ready response, and reddened once again at this arrogant man's audacity in challenging his thoughts. His friends sneered at Thomas in disapproval, and Thomas decided that very instant that enough was enough.

'I am glad you interrupted our proceedings once again, Edmund. I feel this would now be the perfect opportunity to bring up an important matter.'

Edmund's ears pricked up intently, knowing he would not enjoy the words that were about to come from Thomas' mouth.
'It has become absolutely clear that none of you four gentlemen are able to control your outbursts or follow the rules of our society. Our protocols have been structured to allow a reasoned flow of thought, without interruption. You have continually proven your inability to become a part of our group, as you insist on disrupting proceedings despite our many warnings.'

Edmund had murder in his eyes. He was deathly still and silent, staring coldly at Thomas as he continued.

'Your pleas for entry to our club were heard and approved. You were invited to join us many months ago on a trial basis, but we must now conclude from your behaviour that you are not suitable members for our gathering.'

Edmund was turning purple, and if he had been armed with a pistol, Thomas was sure he would have shot him right there and then. Fortunately, he only had his wits to defend him, and Thomas knew they were severely blunted.

'Is this group not supposed to operate as a democracy, sir?' Thomas Gage, another of the troublemakers, spoke up on Edmund's behalf.

'Indeed, you are correct, sir. It fell to me to give you the bad news, but the decision is unanimous. We will put it to the floor for your satisfaction, however.'

To prove his point, and to finally be done with this ugly business, Thomas called the vote there and then.

'All those in favour of non-admittance to the four new prospects, raise your hand and say nay.'
All hands but those of the four rose to a great chorus of 'nay'.

'All those in favour of admittance raise your hand and say aye.' The room was silent, and the four men stared bloody murder at the rest of the group. They began to shake with rage and humiliation. This was an experience they had never endured before. These lowborn people were supposed to feel honoured to have them in their ranks.

'The nayes have it,' Thomas concluded coldly.

The group now stared silently at the pompous prigs, who looked like they were about to have fits. They were spoiled children in the bodies of grown men, and it seemed they were preparing for mighty tantrums.

'The Grand Master will hear of this, you insolent curs!' Burke shouted. 'Come, brothers, let us be away from this common filth!'

They salvaged no dignity as they made their way to the door, spitting curses and hatred as they passed the seated members. The men did not respond.

'You've not heard the last of this, Paine!' cried Edmund. 'You will rue this day, sir!'

'No, sir!' Thomas shouted back as the door swung slowly shut behind them. 'I most certainly will not!'

Epilogue…

In the following months, Thomas' marriage to Elizabeth began to fall apart. Thomas was preoccupied with academic pursuits that Elizabeth was not a party to, and she tired of her lonely existence. Thomas moved to London shortly thereafter, and took up lodgings with Clio while he finished writing his latest work. It was titled The Rights of Man, and posited that popular political revolution was permissible when a government did not safeguard its people's natural rights. At this time, the ruling classes were indeed beginning to fear a revolution, so they suppressed his work and issued a writ for his arrest. Thomas fled to France, but was nonetheless captured there a year later.

He used his time in prison well, composing another great work entitled The Age of Reason, which promoted free thought and argued heavily against institutionalised religion. It destroyed the case for the monarchy, the aristocracy and the corrupted system of the British government, and became one of the most popular works of the time, quickly finding its way back to England's southern shores. The British government prosecuted anyone who published or distributed it.

Thomas was released from prison a year later on the pleas of the American minister to France, James Monroe. Paine became convinced that George Washington had conspired with the British monarchy to have him arrested, and his future looked grim until he had a fortuitous encounter with another great man named Benjamin Franklin. Franklin convinced him to move to America, and provided him with letters of introduction to aid him in the beginnings of a new life on distant shores.

Across the ocean, the American people were becoming concerned and disgusted with the tyranny taking hold in their country. Thomas' newest work, Common Sense, was distributed far and wide and began a truly revolutionary era. Paine quickly became a significant figure in the American Revolution, and it was little surprise to Thomas that once he had settled in that new land and joined the ranks of the patriots, he found himself opposing a loyalist by the name of Thomas Gage. Gage had followed him all the way from Lewes, halfway across the world, under the orders of his brotherhood.

Thirteen great men, including Thomas Paine, gathered together at the end of that war. Together, they penned and signed one of the most important documents ever written, the Declaration of Independence, which stands as the supreme, unamendable, moral law of the United States of America to this very day.

Thirty Third Degree
Masonic Order Meeting
Year 1896

Thirty Third Degree Masonic Order Meeting Year 1896

'Why did we create the cut at Hamsey if we were never going to be able to make use of it?' The Cardinal looked confused. 'Surely somebody will soon notice it would never have been fit for the purpose we suggested it was created for? Would it not have been better to leave it as it was?'

'It suited our needs at the time, brother.' The Grand Master looked at him with aged, dead eyes. 'The cut created only one point of entry to the church by land. After the sea receded and larger boats were no longer able to navigate up the estuary, it gave us the perfect excuse to drastically alter the landscape under the pretence of aiding the population. Now the church is all but forgotten, Hamsey is described as an island, and the Ouse is a narrow river. People have forgotten how far the sea once came inland, and our secrets have become safer than they have ever been, but we must be vigilant. Do not fear the details, brother, the general public are blind sheep, both ignorant and gullible, but the population is growing fast now. We must remain one step ahead of the masses.'

The Grand Master surveyed the room as he sat icily still in his ceremonial robes, daring anyone to meet his eyes. He was frustrated that the secret they had kept for so long was now under threat, and deeply suspicious of betrayal within his organisation. The lodge hall was mostly empty, with only the Shadow King Grand Master and the twelve men of the elite council attending to discuss a concerning issue. Many prominent men had travelled from as far as America and Rome.

'We must now take steps to further control the majority of the information being released to the populace, and we must do it fast. Our present network is far too small for our needs. We require a new brotherhood, gentlemen, a secret army of people on the ground working on our behalf, behind the scenes of every business we can effectively infiltrate, and we will offer great benefits to any who are willing to do so.'

'You are suggesting we recruit spies, Grand Master?' asked the Archbishop, confused.

The Grand Master stared him down, and his cold black eyes had the desired effect. The Archbishop reddened and looked away.

'Not spies, Archbishop, recruits to a secondary secret order. A hidden army working on our behalf and keeping a keen eye and ear out for anything we may need to know of. Might I remind you of what is at stake here?' He screamed the last, slamming his fist down on the arm of the grotesquely grand chair, hoping his anger would quell any further discussion regarding the obvious lie. 'We have been betrayed in the past, and those damn infiltrators have left us with problems that must be solved, and we must solve them now!'

He glared at them again and they all averted their eyes from his gaze.

'We took ownership of ten of the twelve London newspapers over a century ago, and we now have control of many of the provincial papers, but some are proving problematic. We may be forced to take more extreme measures if they do not acquiesce. We must take control of the mainstream narrative, and we must do it quickly!' He paused and scanned the room slowly. Still no-one met his eyes.

'Our second problem is regarding the tomb at Hamsey. Now that Poussin's image of it has circulated around the damn world, it is only a matter of time before somebody else recognises it. It saddens me greatly, but we must remove it, gentlemen.'

'We cannot!' blared the Archbishop, a sudden flash of his usual arrogant demeanour returning briefly to his face.

'Do not forget who you are talking to, Archbishop!' the Grand Master screamed back quickly. 'Mind your tone or you will be excluded from this meeting. I will not warn you again. Do I make myself clear?'

The Archbishop's bravery vanished, subsumed by his innate cowardice, and he turned away, chastened. The Grand Master continued, but did not release his gaze from him.

'When the time is right, the tomb will be deconstructed and stored. It can be rebuilt as a simple altar inside the church sometime in the future, once we have decided how to suitably disguise it. There will be no debate on the matter. We must erase any Templar markings left behind and remove all mention of the de Saye tomb from the record. Somebody will connect him to the Templar Order very soon if we do not act with haste. The walls inside the church will be whitewashed. Fortunately, we had the foresight to build the new church to serve the people in Offham. The fewer services we hold at Old St Peter's from this day forward, the better. We will close the church completely to undertake the work, and ensure that none approach it for many years once it is done. In a generation, what we have done there will fade into forgotten history. We will then begin to place information of our own making into the public record, and before long, Old St Peter's will become a forgotten relic. We will spread word on the smallpox outbreak, on the plague, on the misery and death that occurred there, and fear will also become our ally. If we proceed correctly, people will forget the old port's significance, and we will let them. Once we have completed the work, we will place a loyal servant nearby for time immemorial, to protect the land and the secrets held there. If we do not take control of the situation right now, I fear we will live to regret it very soon, so make it happen! Now, are there any other matters to discuss?'

Bush, a grizzled man in his later years, spoke up. 'I do not wish to add to our troubles, Grand Master, but the damn archaeologists are poking around freely where we do not want them digging. They are already discovering much that will draw attention to the area. A certain Mr Welch has been documenting the vast amount of Anglo-Saxon burials in the hills surrounding Lewes, and he is not willing to join our ranks. I feel it is high time we force our control over these men, and begin to hide the remains of the burial mounds surrounding the town; they will bring much attention to Hamsey and the county in the years to come. We must also find a way for any artefacts discovered in these lands to come to us before they reach a museum. We can then hide them as we see fit, and downplay the importance of the area by controlling the archaeological record. It would be wise to recruit the wealthier of the landowners in the locality to high positions in this secondary organisation. If we make them feel powerful and valued, we will be able to utilise them to serve our needs. They will then guard the land and its lesser secrets on our behalf. Once we have taken control of the narrative, the general public will unwittingly repeat whatever we tell them, but we must be ready to jump on any discoveries that are made in these lands and to keep those finds from making their way to the British Museum. To this end, construction of a golf course on top of Malling Hill is now underway, and this should suitably disguise many of the larger archaeological features left up there. It is with great regret that many of the burial mounds will have to be destroyed, but they will draw far too much attention to the land if they are not removed from view.'

The twelve brothers all nodded and murmured their approval.

'It is agreed, brother,' nodded the Grand Master. 'You have all of our means at your disposal so, once again, make it happen, and keep me informed of your progress. This meeting is adjourned. Bring me the transcripts within the hour. So mote it be!'

'So mote it be,' they echoed in return.

The Grand Master left the room and the twelve Hospitallers breathed a sigh of relief. He was a twisted and dangerous man, and they were all under his thrall. They were cowards, but in death they would be judged and they would all be found wanting.

Epilogue…

That same year, the construction of Lewes golf course began and, one by one, the great burial mounds of the past were quickly pillaged and destroyed. Great efforts were made to disguise any remaining archaeological features, and much of the known history was removed from the public record. In a generation, most had forgotten anything of interest. Maps were drastically altered in the area. The small, ancient island in the centre of the old Ouse estuary was removed from satellite imagery but still remains there to see with your own eyes to this day.

When the railway bridge that had been constructed to disguise the old Roman bridge at Hamsey collapsed, the demolition crews moved in exceptionally fast to remove the remaining evidence. On the Telscombe Tye, the greatest tragedy of all occurred when, once again under the guise of helping the people, a water reservoir was constructed which utterly destroyed Beornwulf's barrow. Nothing was reported on what was found there, just a brief mention of a crouched skeleton and some other interments – proud men who had decided to travel on to the afterlife with Beornwulf and who had deserved a better fate than grave robbery.

The incredible treasures that may have been stolen from Beornwulf, the country and its people there that day can only be speculated on now.

John F Kennedy
Year 1963

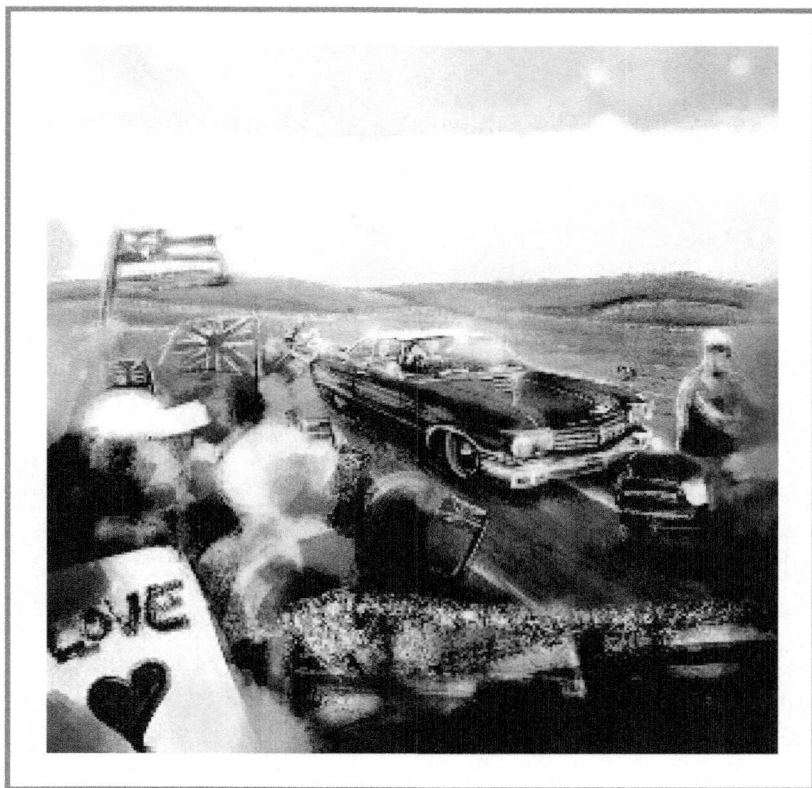

Chapter - 19

John F Kennedy
Year 1963

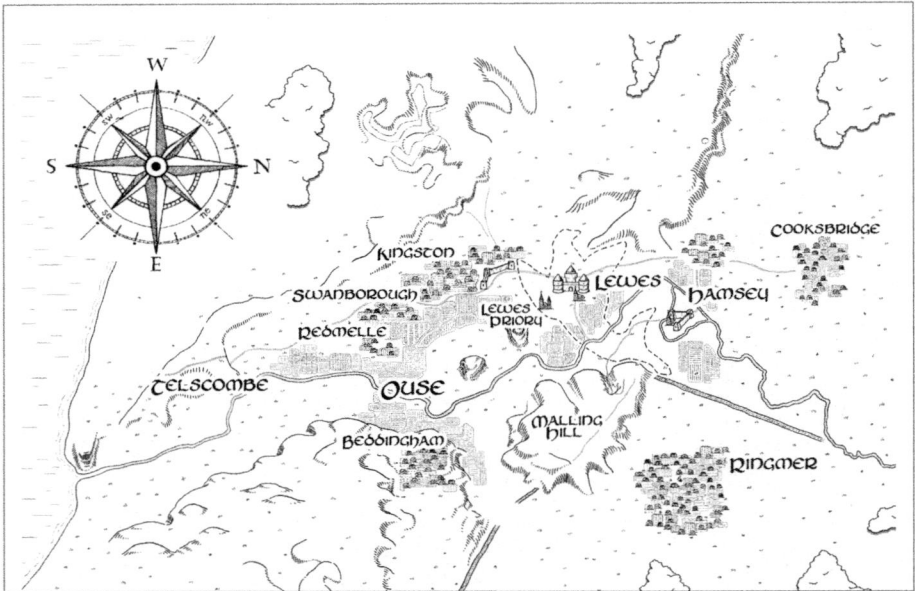

John Kennedy sat quietly in the black Cadillac as it cruised along the narrow country roads of Sussex. He was feeling deeply uneasy, but was trying hard to keep his poker face. The man he thought he had known as a trustworthy ally and friend had just revealed himself to be part of a disturbing secret society he had known absolutely nothing about. What he had just shown him beneath Hamsey Church had torn his world apart. It had come as a genuine shock to a man who thought himself thoroughly in the know when it came to matters of state and international secrets.

It had come to light that, during their lifetime, each of the thirteen members of a disturbing cabal he had just been made aware of had been quietly pulling strings behind the scenes of all the central governments in the world, and their forebears had been keeping the same tradition for centuries. This group of well-placed individuals were somehow connected to the ancient Order of the Knights Hospitaller, and they had now petitioned him to join their cause. It seemed that those thirteen men had been keeping the secret of Christianity's true origins, and had used that secret, the wealth of the Templars and the wealth of the church to place themselves in positions of power, hidden from the masses for close to twelve hundred years. John was struggling to process it all. He had always been a devout practising Catholic, and now his faith in what he thought he knew as fact had been shaken to its core. Not only had many of his beliefs just been shattered, but his strong faith in democracy had also been torn apart, and it was not sitting comfortably with him.

Harold Macmillan puffed on a cigarette and flicked the ash out of the partially opened window. He could read the deep confusion hidden behind Kennedy's blank face, and he understood how he felt. It had been much the same for him when he had first been made aware of the society.

'It gets easier, John,' he said as he inhaled a long draw of smoke and blew it out of the window. 'It takes time to process it all, but it does get easier.'

Kennedy turned to Macmillan and smiled, but his eyes did not reflect the action. In his heart he felt deeply betrayed, and he doubted very much that the feeling would change. The fair world he had always fought for and believed in was now crumbling inside his tired mind.

'I will need a lot of time to process all this, Harold,' he replied in slow, measured tones. He turned his head away to look out of the window.

As they passed a row of copper beech trees on either side of the road, Kennedy reflected on how beautiful this part of the world was. It was so green and unspoiled. So full of age and history. He had begun to love England, and had enjoyed his visit to Birch Grove, but now he just wished to be away from here and back in the familiar territory of home.

Harold felt somewhat ashamed of himself for inflicting this secret knowledge on a man he had become deeply fond of. The pain in Kennedy was palpable.

'I have my concerns too, John,' he impressed on him. 'Much of what I know does not sit easily with me, and I confess much of what is decided upon does not feel honourable any more. I am becoming ever more convinced that a great corruption has worked its way inside our order and is now ruling from the top. I fear some members may have meddled with dark forces far beyond their understanding. It seems there is an evil at work amongst them and I am not sure if I have the power to stop it alone.' He flicked his cigarette end out of the window and rubbed his palms into his eyes as he struggled to find the words to explain.

'I petitioned to bring you into our cause as a last resort, John. The cabal leaders are feeling threatened by you; if I had not attempted to bring you in, I feared they would take more drastic action. Your speech on secret societies and your political success does not fit well with their plans. They have spent centuries blending into the background of society, and do not like attention being drawn to their existence.'

Kennedy turned to face him, with no trace of friendliness behind his gaze. 'And how did you find yourself drawn into this cabal, Harold?' He stared him down with angry, accusing eyes.

Harold turned away from his withering glare. 'It's not a simple matter, John.' He paused as he gathered his thoughts. 'I came from nothing, and spent a lifetime attempting to better myself. I worked hard to get ahead in life and I joined a society called the Order of the Buffaloes when I was very young. I was recruited by them, and I felt privileged to have been asked. It felt good to finally be on the inside track, and life quickly got better for me and my family once I had become a member. I became very wealthy through our society's contact base and, as a young man, the feeling of having "one up" on the majority of the world was more intoxicating than anything I had known. It is a strangely powerful position to find yourself in, but I now worry that many ill-minded members have let their protection go too far. I know, and have known, many men who, without the backing of the society, would otherwise be behind bars. Some of them now have a true air of evil about them that I cannot condone. They have become a law unto themselves. The Order now has great influence globally, and there is almost no situation that they cannot bribe or threaten their way out of. It has become a corrupted world of illusion, John, and the infection runs very deep.' He paused again to gather his thoughts. He was not sure if he should carry on with his confession, but he had come this far, and he truly cared what Kennedy thought of him, so he continued.

'This is going to be very hard to explain, but to understand what is really going on in the world, I will have to talk to you of things that you will not find easy to accept, but accept them or not, you will soon come to see that what I tell you is a great truth. The question is, do you really want to know, John? You will never see the world in the same way again if I tell you these things.'

Kennedy looked at Macmillan with a quizzical look on his face. 'There is more?' he asked, confounded.

'We've not even scratched the surface,' Macmillan replied. 'There are other, ancient secrets that are simple in essence, but very difficult to explain. Your current mindset may not allow you to believe what I say, but it is certainly within your power to understand the concepts.'

He paused, waiting, and Kennedy nodded for him to continue.

'Many centuries ago, the founding members of the Order realised that the greatest power above all other powers is simply held within a story. As strange as it may sound, they then seized upon the power of the greatest story of our time – the Holy Bible.'

Kennedy's face could not hide his scepticism, but he motioned for Harold to continue.

'For those who have the ears to hear, let him hear…' quoted Macmillan, shaking his head. 'This may be hard to accept for you, John, but the Holy Bible is all written as both a translation of metaphoric and actual events. Life itself is a type of symbiotic biological metaphor. As you are now aware, Jesus truly existed and he was a human being, just like everybody else.

There was one very important difference, however; he was a rare breed of man who discovered that the one true God was within himself. "God" was a part of his very own self.'

Kennedy looked incredulous, but Macmillan continued.

'The man, Jesus, then attempted to help everyone realise that same truth; to break them free from the bondage of what they had been conditioned to believe, to give them the courage to follow their own story. That knowledge did not serve the Roman Empire, however, so the Bible was altered and oppressed by greedy men of the church who had also become aware of this secret, and sought to profit and control the populace with this knowledge instead of using it to set them free. Bible stories were written as metaphors to make the mind grow, to force you to work out the deeper, double meanings in everything for yourself.'

Kennedy still looked unconvinced, but Macmillan could see he was also beginning to gain his interest.

'All throughout history, people have been looking outside of themselves for their knowledge and their truth. Consequently, they have given all their attention, confidence and power to the words and ideas of others. Due to this fundamental flaw, they continually expect to find their knowledge and truth in the minds of others, and where do you think those people got their ideas? You see, humanity has two underlying problems. The first is a deep need to seek assurance outside of themselves, and the second is a serious lack of focus. It takes keen attention and a willingness to deconstruct old belief patterns, but one day, as more and more people work towards shedding their old certainties, they will realise that not only do they contain the power to create their own reality, but that they have been living in someone else's story, a story that has been fed to them their whole life, a story they have taken as gospel truth and replayed in their minds as fact since the day they were born. A story they were not even aware they were a part of.'

'How can that possibly be true, Harold?' questioned Kennedy in disbelief.

'Although most people are not aware of it, our subconscious creates and holds our personal truths, and they in turn dictate our personal realities. It is a horrifying thought to process, John, but around eighty percent of all news, film, television and information across the world at this time is fabricated to fit the agenda of the cabal. The thirteen are fully aware that mass thought manipulation eventually congeals itself into fact, for in the words of Frederick Nietzsche, "What is truth, but a lie agreed upon?" Whatever stories are received by a populace – old or new, fact or fiction – play out for them in some way if they are given enough emotional investment; how could they not? Now, if someone else controls the vast majority of the information put out to the public, they in turn have power over mass perception and can manipulate human behaviour as they see fit. People are unaware of this terrifying truth, simply because they have not paid enough attention to what occurs in their past, their present and their future. If they had, they would see that their lives are just unconscious living metaphors; repetitions of old stories they are told and then tell themselves about who they are and how things are. I have often wondered if that is where the idea of purgatory has come from. You see, people tend to manifest what they subconsciously are in life, not what they want to be. We simply suffer ourselves and our personal truths lifetime after lifetime, but in a nutshell, everyone has always had the power and freedom to create their own beliefs, to be their own God.' Macmillan held up a finger to stem Kennedy's incredulity. 'This does not mean you become all powerful and omnipotent, as some may assume, you simply understand in the depths of your being that you are a part of God and so is everything else, and that while you are here on Earth, you have an incredible opportunity to learn and to create. Sadly, most will never seek this truth, and of those that do, many will still not find it.'

'This is hard to swallow,' said Kennedy, as Harold tapped out another Woodbine from his cigarette packet, struck a match and took a long draw. He wiped his brow, flicked the ash out of the window and continued.

'It is, John, but I understand your scepticism, so let me elaborate. Let us see if you still feel the same way once you have heard me out to the end?'

Kennedy nodded his agreement.

'Have you ever noticed that the symbol of a pinecone is found in nearly all of the religions in the world? And have you ever noticed that they all occur irrespective of one another?'

Kennedy shook his head. He had always been a devout Catholic and had not given much attention to other religious practices, but he did know of the Fontella Della Pigna in Vatican City.

'The pinecone and the eye are common symbols found in every religion since the beginning of the written record; the all-seeing eye is even on the dollar bill and has not been printed there by accident, just like a head on a penny. They are absolutely everywhere, and countless enlightened individuals have explained this symbology, yet humanity does not choose to see, or to listen. The pinecone symbolises the pineal gland. It is a small gland which is roughly the same shape as a pinecone, located in the centre of the brain. It is also known as the third eye. When an individual experiences a heightened activation of that third eye, they become aware that God is, and always has been, within them; working through and alongside their own consciousness. This expansion of awareness is what is known as enlightenment. There are various routes available to attain this realisation, but it is a slow process to achieve safely and as people get older and more certain of their beliefs, it gets harder and harder to achieve. You see, if the mind is not flexible enough to accept new possibilities, it will crack apart and only lead to madness. So half the battle in attaining this realisation is in shedding old certainties, but sadly, people cling fiercely to their old beliefs. They do not like to have their concrete views of the world challenged.'

Kennedy nodded his agreement, and Macmillan continued.

'It is interesting to note that every act of hatred ever perpetrated in this world has been committed in the name of one person's belief over another person's belief, and all because of self-inflicted, secondhand doctrine. It is a madness, is it not? What so few people seem to understand is that belief in anything outside of their personal experience is just that, simply a belief in some secondhand information they have read or heard, most of which is designed to lead people to an outcome that they did not choose, or even consider possible. It would seem that, all throughout history, each member of humanity has had a desperate need to feel that they know "the truth" and would have everyone believe the same as them, but it is without a doubt that what is true for one person is not necessarily true for another, is it not?'

Kennedy nodded his agreement once again.

'And yet there are common themes that run unconsciously throughout large groups of human life, and if you had studied other religions, you would find it is no accident that all of the great saints and sages of the past have been telling their own version of exactly the same story since the beginning of the written record. Those stories are all a metaphor for the underlying processes occurring within the mind, body and spirit of man, which is mirrored in the very cosmos itself.'

He paused to consider how far down the rabbit hole he could lead John before his mind would really start to rebel against what he was telling him.

'Have you ever noticed how the theme of thirteen men reoccurs in many of the great stories of our past, John?'

Kennedy raised a quizzical eyebrow and shook his head.

'There is always a leader and twelve others. Kronos and the twelve Olympians, Jesus and his twelve disciples, King Arthur and his twelve Knights. Charlemagne and the twelve peers, or "Paladins". Beowulf and his twelve warriors. The signatories of the Declaration of Independence. Even Adolf Hitler worked out that he needed twelve "apostles" to be an effective force in the world.'

Kennedy looked alarmed and a little uneasy as he realised that Harold was right; he was also stunned that he had not noticed this before.

'You see, John, man has spent many years observing the universe; the cycles of the moon, the sun and the other planets. Those planetary bodies tell a mathematical story of their own, which reflects itself in our physical reality and in our subconscious. The same themes that play out in the heavens also play out within us, and that spreads throughout the world as creation. To continue with this example, there are twelve months in a year, twelve hours on a clock face, twelve signs of the zodiac, the twelve tribes of Israel, the twelve days of Christmas, the book of the twelve… I could go on. What is important to note is that the twelve individual sections make up the whole.'

Macmillan gave Kennedy some time to process what he had just told him. He was beginning to look deeply confused, so Macmillan decided not to go on much further.

'There are many other mathematical processes playing out in daily life too, but I do not want to overwhelm your mind with too much new information all at once, so we will keep on this track for now. What is important to understand is that once a story takes hold of man, it permeates through the collective human subconscious and then manifests itself into reality over and over again. So the people who are truly in control of the world are simply the best storytellers of the ages, who are often found, either consciously or unconsciously, to be working from the mathematical framework of the greatest stories of our past. I fear it is a great tragedy that news outlets have become today's storytellers for the masses, and I find it strange that bad news sells more than good, do you not agree, John?' He did not give Kennedy the time to reply. 'It does not speak well of us. People just do not seem to see it, but as long as they choose to give their attention to negativity and the ideas of others, they will continue to be unconsciously controlled by them; they will always remain trapped in someone else's story, a story that is an attention-grabbing, fear-inducing, miserable version of reality, but one that, strangely, they choose to believe in willingly. Now, John, if being unconsciously trapped in somebody else's version of reality is not Hell, then I do not know what is, and I dread to think what may occur if our growing technology ever manages to connect the whole world to the same information. If people would just gather their own groups of twelve together and form their own communities based not on greed, but on their own ideals of happiness, the world would be a far better place, but we must always remember that one man's greed can ruin the world, John. The greedy ones are the greatest enemies to mankind.'

Kennedy held up his hand. 'Please, Harold, you will have to let me process this for a while. I feel like I am losing a grip on my own reality, and it is most unsettling. I will need to think on all of this for some time.'

Harold nodded his understanding, and they spent the remainder of their journey in uncomfortable silence.

Epilogue…

Kennedy spent the night at Birch Grove. Despite having had his own bed flown in for him, his back ached, his mind rebelled and he barely slept a wink. In the morning, he attended a mass in Forest Row with Macmillan, and despite a minority group of 'Ban the Bomb' protestors, he was very well received. Later that day, after a joint discussion, they agreed that a nuclear test ban treaty was essential. Having completed his duties, Kennedy boarded a helicopter and flew off into the great valley of the Weald. He landed at Gatwick, and was mightily relieved to board the presidential plane and fly home.

Just five months later in Dallas, on November 22, 1963, he was assassinated in an open-topped car on his way to a trade mart. Unusually, his route had been widely reported in newspapers days before the event, and yet when the assassin took his shots, the motorcade was not where it was supposed to be. Kennedy had been taken on a new route. A route that led him straight to his death.

Kennedy had made a speech on secret societies at the Waldorf-Astoria Hotel, New York City, in 1961.

"The very word secrecy is repugnant in a free and open society; and we are as a people inherently and historically opposed to secret societies, to secret oaths and to secret proceedings. And there is a very grave danger that an announced need for increased security will be seized upon by those anxious to expand its meaning to the very limits of official censorship and concealment. And so it is to the printing press – to the recorder of man's deeds, the keeper of his conscience, the courier of his news – that we look for strength and assistance, confident that, with your help, man will be what he was born to be: free and independent."

George Jones
Year 2018

Chapter - 20

George Jones
Year 2018

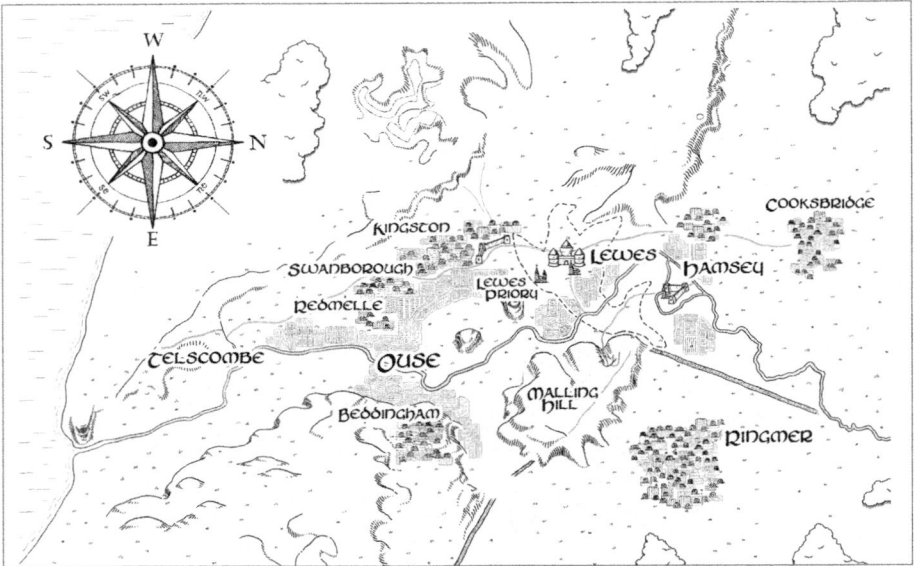

George hung up the phone after speaking to the extremely helpful lady at the British Museum. He had just been informed that no metal detecting finds from Lewes had been handed in to the museum for over twenty years. George found that rather unlikely given the numbers of detectorists he had seen in the area. It was now the third time he had become aware of something untoward occurring in the county with regards to its archaeology, and he was beginning to get a sense that something extraordinary was being covered up there. George decided that day, to look into it a little further...

Printed in Great Britain
by Amazon